As Mia turned quickly to see who was there the ladder swung backwards and sent her flying through the air with a terrified scream.

Ryan caught her just before she hit the floor, absorbing the impact of her fall.

Mia gasped.

He was still holding her close and made no reply, just kept looking down on her. It was the first time he'd held a woman like this since he'd lost Beth and it was gut wrenching. He'd always known it would be, and had made sure that it never happened for his sanity's sake, but with Mia it was as if he just couldn't avoid her. She was everywhere he turned and he didn't want it to be like that.

Putting her carefully back on to her feet, he said abruptly. 'Whatever possessed you to try something so dangerous as painting this high ceiling? You should have hired a decorator.'

'It would be too expensive,' she replied, wishing those moments in his arms had affected him as much as they'd affected her. She'd felt safe and protected as he'd held her close, and it seemed like a lifetime since she'd last had those sorts of feelings.

Dear Reader

Would you like to come with me to a small and enchanting market town to read about the lives and loves of a charismatic man who thinks he has all his priorities right—until he meets a beautiful woman whose life has become a hurtful catastrophe due to the unkindness of others?

If so, do please read on.

With best wishes

Abigail Gordon

CHRISTMAS MAGIC IN HEATHERDALE

BY
ABIGAIL GORDON

First published in Great Britain 2013
by Mills & Boon, an imprint of Harlequin (UK) Limited.
Harlequin (UK) Limited, Eton House, 18-24 Paradise Road,
Richmond, Surrey TW9 1SR

© Abigail Gordon 2013

ISBN: 978 0 263 23569 2

Harlequin (UK) policy is to use papers that are natural, renewable and recyclable products and made from wood grown in sustainable forests. The logging and manufacturing process conform to the legal environmental regulations of the country of origin.

Printed and bound in Great Britain
by CPI Antony Rowe, Chippenham, Wiltshire

Abigail Gordon loves to write about the fascinating combination of medicine and romance from her home in a Cheshire village. She is active in local affairs, and is even called upon to write the script for the annual village pantomime! Her eldest son is a hospital manager, and helps with all her medical research. As part of a close-knit family, she treasures having two of her sons living close by, and the third one not too far away. This also gives her the added pleasure of being able to watch her delightful grandchildren growing up.

Recent titles by the same author:

SWALLOWBROOK'S WEDDING OF THE YEAR
MARRIAGE MIRACLE IN SWALLOWBROOK**
SPRING PROPOSAL IN SWALLOWBROOK**
SWALLOWBROOK'S WINTER BRIDE**
SUMMER SEASIDE WEDDING†
VILLAGE NURSE'S HAPPY-EVER-AFTER†
WEDDING BELLS FOR THE VILLAGE NURSE†
CHRISTMAS IN BLUEBELL COVE†
COUNTRY MIDWIFE, CHRISTMAS BRIDE*

***The Doctors of Swallowbrook Farm*
**The Willowmere Village Stories*
†*Bluebell Cove*

Did you know these are also available as eBooks?
Visit www.millsandboon.co.uk

For Robert Bonar,
a good friend and the kindest of men.

CHAPTER ONE

EMPLOYED AS A paediatric consultant at Heatherdale Children's Hospital, Ryan Ferguson was used to the demands of the job, but today had been in a class of its own. Relieved to finally be away from work he pulled up outside the elegant town house that was home to him and his two small daughters.

Rhianna and Martha would be fast asleep at this late hour, but he was grateful that they would have been tucked up for the night by Mollie, his kindly house-keeper, who in spite of the time would have a meal waiting for him.

Ryan's work centred mainly on children with neu-rological illnesses and injuries and his dedication to his calling was an accepted fact by all who knew him. His intention to bring up his children as a single father was more of a surprise, as there were many women who would be only too willing to fill the gap in his life.

Today's non-stop problems had been serious and in some cases rare, with almost a certainty that the dreaded meningitis would be lurking somewhere amongst his young patients and the battle to overthrow it would begin.

With the workload as heavy as it was, it was becoming obvious that they needed another registrar on the neuro unit to assist him and Julian Tindall, his second-in-command.

A rare shortage of nursing staff due to a bug that had been going round hadn't helped, and as he'd performed his daily miracles the hours had galloped past. Now he was ready to put the day's stresses to the back of his mind and enjoy the warmth and peace of his home for a few hours. Home was in the delightful small spa town of Heatherdale, tucked away amongst the rugged peaks and smooth green dales of the countryside, with Manchester being the nearest big city.

The moment he was out of the car and had collected his briefcase from the back seat he moved swiftly towards where warmth and hot food would be waiting for him, casting a brief glance in the direction of the property next to it as he did so, and his step slowed.

A town house like his own, it had been empty for years and he was amazed to see a car parked outside and a flicker of light coming from inside, as if from a torch or a candle. He frowned. He doubted it was thieves, as there would be nothing in there to steal. Could be squatters, though, and the thought was not appealing.

When his housekeeper opened the door to him she couldn't wait to tell him the latest neighbourhood news. When she'd returned from picking the children up from school there had been the car parked outside, and shortly afterwards a bed had been delivered from a nearby furniture store.

'Wow!' he exclaimed as he closed the door behind him. 'Surely they've had it cleaned first? It must be filthy after being empty for so many years. The amount of lighting inside has to mean that they've not had the electricity switched on and are using candles or a torch. It seems an odd state of affairs. Once I've changed into something less formal, I'll do the neighbourly thing and go and introduce myself, ask if there is anything I can assist them with.'

When he knocked on the door of the run-down house that was a blight in the crescent of much-admired Victorian town houses there was no sound for a moment. Then the door swung open slowly and his jaw dropped at the sight of a slender stranger with long dark hair that swung gently against her shoulders and a face blotched with weeping.

'They haven't been,' she cried desperately as he was on the point of introducing himself. 'The cleaners haven't been and the place is full of spiders' webs and the dust of years. I will have to find a hotel for the night.'

'Are you alone here?' he asked carefully. 'I'm Ryan Ferguson, and my family and I are your new neighbours.' He held out his hand in greeting. The tearful stranger shook it limply but didn't volunteer any information about herself. She seemed extremely distracted, which was no wonder considering the situation.

He got the impression that she wanted him gone but he could hardly go back to his own comfortable home and leave her in such a state.

'Can you recommend a hotel not too far away?' she asked. 'I just can't spend the night in here. I've had a bed delivered but haven't taken the wrappings off it so it should come to no harm for the present.'

Ryan was still standing in the doorway and would have liked to see just what a mess the inside of the house was in, but he could hardly go barging in without an invite.

'You must be exhausted. I'll take you to a hotel if you would like to lock up. My car is parked out front like yours, so I will lead the way and you can follow.'

'Thank you,' she said unsteadily. 'I do apologise for breaking into your evening. I shall be onto the cleaners first thing in the morning.'

'I'm only too pleased to be of assistance,' he told her. 'If you will just give me a moment, I'll go and get my car keys.'

When Mollie opened the door to him again he explained, 'This is our new neighbour, Mollie. I'm taking her to a hotel as the house isn't quite ready to move into.'

'Oh, you poor dear,' Mollie said, observing the strange woman standing hesitantly at the kerb edge. 'What a horrible thing to happen, and on a cold, dark night like this.' She turned to Ryan. 'I'm just about to dish up your meal before I go home for the day. There's plenty to spare, so can we not offer the young lady some hospitality?'

'Yes, of course, by all means,' he said, forgetting his weariness for a moment.

Their new neighbour shrank back.

'I couldn't possibly intrude into your evening any more than I am doing,' she said.

Ignoring her reluctance, Ryan insisted. 'You are most welcome. How long is it since you last had something to eat?'

'I can't remember.'

'If that's the case, you need food now.' He stepped back to let her past him to where Mollie was hovering near the kitchen door. 'If you want to wash your hands you'll find anything you need in the cloakroom at the end of the hall. Mollie will have the food on the table when you're done.'

'Thank you,' she croaked meekly, and disappeared.

Mollie was ready to go by the time his unexpected guest had removed the day's surface grime and once they were alone silence descended in what was a tastefully furnished dining room.

When they'd finished eating Ryan said, 'There's a fire in the sitting room. Make yourself comfortable while I make coffee.'

She nodded and said uncomfortably, 'The food was lovely. Thank you so much.'

He was observing her gravely. 'Are you going to tell me who you are? The house next door has been unoccupied for many years so it was a surprise to find signs of life there when I came home. Are you actually planning to live there?'

'Er, yes,' she told him hesitantly. 'My name is Melissa Redmond. The house was left to me by my grandmother when she died some years ago. I've had no interest in living out here in the backwoods until a short time ago when my circumstances changed dramatically.

'I'd arranged for a firm of cleaners to come in and make it liveable, and for the power to be connected, but when I got here late this afternoon nothing had been done and I was frantic.'

'Yes, I can understand that,' Ryan said slowly. Melissa didn't look quite as bedraggled in the warm glow of the lamps in his sitting room as she had when she'd opened the door of the mausoleum next door. The colour had returned to her cheeks and she seemed a lot calmer. His curiosity about his new neighbour had definitely been piqued. He wanted to know more.

When he came back with the coffee cups she was asleep, overcome by the comforting warmth of the fire. So it looked as if he wasn't going to find out any more about her for now.

An hour passed and Melissa hadn't stirred out of the deep sleep of exhaustion that had claimed her. There was no way she could be allowed to go back to the chill of the house that had been empty for so long, neither did Ryan want to rouse her to go to a hotel at that hour. Instead, he went and found a soft fleece, laid it gently over her, and went up to bed with the intention of checking on her at regular intervals. That turned out to be a wise precaution as the first time he went downstairs, she was awake and about to disappear through the front door.

'Melissa, wait!' he cried. 'You can't stay in that place tonight. I have a spare room that is always kept ready for visitors. I insist you stay in it. I won't be able to sleep knowing that you're not somewhere safe, *and* I've had a very exhausting day that I need to recover from before the next one is upon me.'

'My nightwear is in my case next door,' she protested faintly.

'I'll find you some,' he offered. Was he going insane to let a strange woman wear something that had belonged to Beth?

He pointed to a gracious curved staircase and said, 'If you would like to go up, I'll show you to the guest room. While you are settling in there I'll find something for you to wear.'

Ryan dug out one of Beth's plain cotton nightshirts to lend to Melissa. He avoided taking out any of the prettier nightgowns that Beth had favoured.

Melissa took it from him with a subdued smile and said with tears threatening, 'I hope that one day I'll be able to repay your kindness, Ryan.'

He smiled. 'Don't concern yourself about that. Tomorrow is another day and it just has to be better than this one has been for you.'

With that brief word of comfort he left her and went to a room across the landing. Closing the door behind him, he looked down at his sleeping daughters and wondered just what Rhianna and Martha would think when they saw there was a visitor for breakfast.

As she lay sleeplessly under the covers of the bed in the spare room, Melissa's thoughts were in overdrive. The future that had looked so bleak seemed slightly less so because of the kindness of a stranger who had taken her in, fed her, and offered her a bed for the night.

So much for keeping a low profile in her new surroundings! The hurts she had suffered over recent months had made her long for privacy, for somewhere to hide. But her meeting with a man with the golden fairness of a Viking and eyes as blue as a summer sky had put an end to those sorts of plans.

It seemed Ryan had children who no doubt were fast asleep, and was in sole charge of them, so where was their mother? Wherever it might be, it was not her business. She had to fix her thoughts on tomorrow and the cleaners, the electricity people, and accepting the delivery of her few remaining belongings some time during the day. With those thoughts in mind she drifted into an uneasy sleep.

The sound of children's voices on the landing mingling with her host's deeper tones brought Melissa into instant wakefulness in the darkness of a winter morning. She dressed quickly in yesterday's clothes and prepared to go down to where she could hear the sounds of breakfast-time coming from the kitchen.

Pausing in the doorway, she saw that Ryan was at

the grill, keeping an eye on sizzling bacon, and two little girls were seated at the table with bowls of cereal in front of them, observing her with wide eyes of surprise as she said, 'Thank you so much for last night. I feel a different person this morning after the meal and the rest. I'm off to find out what happened to the cleaners and the electricity services.'

He smiled across at her. 'Not before you've eaten. You have no facilities for preparing food next door, so take a seat.'

Rhianna, at seven years old and the elder of his two young daughters, was not a shy child, and burst out, 'Who is this lady, Daddy? She wasn't here when we went to bed.'

'No, she wasn't,' Martha, two years younger, chirped beside her. At that point Ryan took charge of the conversation.

'Her name is Melissa and she's going to live next door to us,' he explained. 'Melissa, these are my daughters, Rhianna and Martha.'

'She can't!' Rhianna protested.

'Why not?' he asked.

'It's haunted!'

'No way,' he said laughingly as he pulled out a chair for Melissa to be seated, as if there had been no hesitation in joining them on her part. 'There aren't any ghosts in Heatherdale, I promise you that, Rhianna. Now, who would like a bacon roll?'

'Me!' the children both cried.

With the day ahead momentarily forgotten, Melissa smiled as the memory surfaced of how, when she'd been at junior school, she and her friends used to pass a creepy-looking empty house on the way there. They had been convinced that there was a human hand on the inside window ledge. It had only been when one of their fathers had gone to investigate that it had been discovered that the 'hand' had been a pink plastic glove. There had been much disappointment amongst the children.

She had done as Ryan requested and seated herself opposite him. As she smiled across at his children she saw that they both had the same golden fairness as their father, but their eyes were different—big and brown and fixed on her.

Making her second contribution to the occasion, Martha asked, 'Are you some children's mummy? We haven't got one any more. Ours was hurt by a tree.'

Ryan had just put cereal and a bacon sandwich in front of Melissa and was about to join them at the table. He stilled, and she saw dismay in his expression.

'Just get on with your breakfast, Martha,' he said gravely, 'and no more questions.'

'It's all right,' Melissa told him. 'I don't mind. They are delightful.' She turned to his small daughter.

'No, Martha, I'm not a mummy, but I do love children. My job is all about making them well when they are sick.'

Their interest was waning to find that she didn't fit their requirements, but not their father's. The stranger at their table was full of surprises. What kind of a job was it that she'd referred to?

Bringing his mind back to their morning routine on school days, when the children had finished eating he told them to go and put their school uniforms on and have their satchels ready for when Mollie came to take them to school.

'Will Melissa be here when we come home?' Rhianna asked.

She answered for Ryan. 'I'm afraid not, Rhianna. My house needs cleaning and sorting. But once that's done everything will be fine and you can come to see me whenever you like.'

Rhianna seemed happy with that answer and she and Martha hopped off to get ready for school.

'Your daughters are adorable, Ryan,' she said with a warm smile.

'They're the light of my life. A life that would not be easy if Mollie wasn't around,' Ryan replied. 'She's a good friend as well as my housekeeper. I have a very demanding job but it's totally rewarding and somehow I manage to give it my best, while organising things at this end to make sure that Rhianna and Martha are happy, though the result is not always how I want it to be. Still, I mustn't delay you. We both have busy days ahead of us.'

She couldn't have agreed more. As she looked around her at his delightful home, the gloom of yesterday came back. Dreading what the day would hold for her, she wished Ryan a stilted goodbye and went to ring the cleaning firm and the electricity company.

As Melissa waited for the cleaners to arrive, her mind drifted back over her recent past. She recalled how only yesterday, stony-faced behind the wheel of her car, she had driven away from the house that had always been her home in a select area of a Cheshire green belt without looking back.

The doors had been locked, the windows shut fast, and as a last knife thrust she'd put flowers in the hall-way, a huge bunch of them that would be the first thing that the new owners saw when they arrived to take over their recently acquired property.

The purchase had been completed early that morn-ing, the money was already in her bank account, but the thought of it brought no joy. It would be a matter of here today and gone tomorrow.

'I'm sorry, sweetheart,' her father had said as the last few moments of his life had ebbed away. 'So sorry to be going like this before I'd sorted things.'

'You have nothing to be sorry for,' she'd told him gently, thinking that he must be delirious. 'You have always been there for me, making me laugh, indulg-ing me, keeping me safe, and David will do the same. I know he will.'

He'd tried to speak again but the mists had been closing in and the nurse at the other side of the bed had said a few seconds later, 'He's gone, Melissa. His injuries were too severe for him to overcome. There will be no more pain for your father.'

Max Redmond had been a charmer, and a wealthy one at that. Melissa had lost her mother to heart failure when she had been eleven and Max had given her everything she could possibly have wanted to make up for the loss. He'd taken her on fantastic holidays, bought her the kind of car that most young people could only dream of when she had been old enough to drive, and had given her a generous allowance that had been more than some families had had to feed their children and pay the mortgage.

The two of them had lived in a smart detached house amongst the rich and famous, not far from the city, and when she'd gone to fulfil a dream and enrolled as a medical student, it had been at a university in nearby Manchester so that her father wouldn't be lonely, although it hadn't seemed likely.

Max had never remarried, but he'd made lots of women friends in the circles in which he'd moved, where wining and dining was the order of the day. However, he had always cancelled any arrangements he'd made if his daughter had been free to socialise with him.

That had been until she'd got engaged to David Lowson, the son of one of her father's women friends. After that, he'd watched benignly as most of Melissa's time away from her career had been taken up with the delights of being in love.

She'd qualified as a doctor in paediatrics in the summer, and on receiving her degree had been employed at a nearby hospital. Life had been good in every way, with all of it centred around the big city that she knew so well and would never have wanted to leave, until her father had walked in front of a speeding car on a road not far from where they lived after a lively lunch in a nearby hotel, and had died from his injuries.

Since then Melissa had experienced all of life's worst emotions: grief at the sudden tragic loss of the man who had loved her so much; sick horror to discover that his last words to her had been referring to a huge mountain of gambling debts that he had accumulated.

There had also been the aching hurt of betrayal from an engagement that had fizzled out when her fiancé had discovered that she was no longer the wealthy heiress that his mother had urged him to propose to, and was going to be poorer than a church mouse by the time she'd sorted out Max's frightening legacy.

Everything Melissa could lay her hands on had been sold, and most of her salary each month had gone into the bottomless pit, with the sale of the house as the final heartbreaking humiliation.

During the time that the sale had been going through, those who knew her had seen little of her. Grief stricken and panicked about the future, Melissa had chosen to hide away from her friends.

Her father had given no inkling that he'd had money problems. Always a man about town, as generous host to all his friends, he hadn't been able to admit to his failings, and she now understood fully his weak apology as he'd lain dying.

Incredibly, there'd been no life insurance to fall back

on, or other safeguards that were usually in place regarding the death of a person, but thankfully the money from the sale of the house would clear the last of the debts.

She supposed it would have been sensible to rent herself a small apartment in Manchester and bring the shattered remnants of her life together again somehow. But with her father now resting with her mother in a nearby cemetery, and an ex-fiancé who had cast her aside living not far away, she had been intent on moving to some place where she wasn't known.

Having left the hospital where she'd been employed, she'd headed for the small market town of Heatherdale, where her paternal grandmother had lived and where her house, which had been empty for a long time, was there for her if she wanted it.

The old lady had willed it to her and, though grateful for the thought, it was the last place she would ever have contemplated moving to in the past, but the present was proving to be a different matter. Alone and lost, she'd needed somewhere to hide from the pitying looks she'd received from her father's friends and acquaintances when the news had got around that she was penniless. She'd wanted somewhere to avoid the mocking smiles of those who had witnessed the plight of the 'golden girl' and thought it would do her good to see how the other half lived. But the thing that had hurt most had been the speed with which her ex had found another woman to replace her.

She had found the keys to her grandmother's house

in a chest of drawers in her father's bedroom, and as she'd gazed down at the heavy ornate bunch of them it had been as if a means of escape was being offered to her.

There had been receipts with them for payments that her father had made to the local authorities on her behalf over the years to comply with the law regarding the ownership of unoccupied housing, and she'd decided that the paperwork and the keys were heaven sent.

She'd felt as if she never wanted to see the city that she'd loved so much, with its familiar shops, smart restaurants and green parks, ever again. She'd decided to make a fresh start in a place that she'd never cared for much on the rare occasions she'd been there.

With no job, no money, and no family, she had to hope that she could find a future for herself in Heatherdale. First she had to get the house straight. Next on her agenda was finding a job. The obvious choice would be its famous hospital, but if there were no vacancies there for a newly qualified paediatrician then she'd simply have to find something to tide her over.

The internet had come up with the name and address of a firm of domestic cleaners in the Heatherdale area and she'd hired them to give the house a thorough cleaning from top to bottom before she arrived.

Apart from ordering a bed to be delivered later in the day, when she would be there to accept it, the rest of her belongings would arrive the following afternoon, when she was satisfied that the house was ready to take delivery of them.

It wasn't the best time of year to be moving into a strange house in a strange place, she'd thought achingly as the miles had flashed past. The last leaves of autumn had been scattered at the roadside or hanging limply on trees, and a cold wind had been nipping at her while she'd been taking a last walk around the gardens of what had been her home.

During her early childhood she and her parents had visited her grandmother occasionally, but there hadn't been any real closeness between them because the old lady had disapproved of her son's attitude to life in general. She hadn't liked the way he'd been such a spendthrift, although at that time he hadn't reached retirement and had been making big money in the stock markets.

'When I die I'm leaving the house to the child,' she'd told him. 'There might come a day when she'll need a roof over her head.' As the lights of Heatherdale had appeared on the horizon, Melissa had reflected that the grandmother she'd rarely seen had turned out to be her only friend.

Martha's innocent question about the stranger who had joined them for breakfast was uppermost in Ryan's mind as he drove the short distance to the hospital. It had brought painful memories with it that he only allowed himself to think about when he was alone, but in that moment in the kitchen they had been starkly clear and he'd been extra-loving with the children while they'd waited for Mollie to arrive.

His youngest daughter had described them as being without a mother because theirs had been hurt by a tree. It wouldn't have been the easiest description of her death for Melissa Redmond to understand, but did that matter? She was just a stranger who had joined them for breakfast.

He and Beth had attended the same school in Heatherdale, had both chosen medicine as a career, he in paediatrics and she in midwifery. It had always been there, the love that had blossomed in their late teens and taken them to the altar of a church in the small market town where they lived.

Heatherdale boasted a famous spa that people came from far and wide to take advantage of, and beautiful Victorian architecture built from local stone that he never wearied of. There were spacious parks and elegant shops and restaurants. Everything that he loved was here except for the wife he had adored.

When she'd died he had wanted to die too as life had lost its meaning, but there had been two small children, unhappy and confused because their mother hadn't been there any more, so he'd pulled himself together for their sakes. In the last three years his life had been entirely taken up with his children and the health problems of those belonging to others.

If it meant that he never had time to do his own thing, at least there was the comfort of knowing that his young daughters were safe and happy, and that he was serving a vital purpose in the Heatherdale Children's Hospital where he was a senior paediatric consultant.

He knew that folks found him irritating at times because he never socialised, was always too busy when
asked out to dine, even though he had Mollie, who
would always take on the role of childminder if needed
and who checked out every available woman she met
as a possible new wife for him, without actually saying so openly.

As Melissa looked around her house in the cold light
of day she was hoping that today would not be quite
as horrendous as yesterday. However, every day since
she'd lost her father and discovered what he had been
involved in had been dreadful.

For the past few weeks she'd felt lost and alone, like
some sort of outcast. Ryan's kindness had been a brief
relief from what had been a nightmare for her, but at
the same time getting involved with anyone at the moment was the last thing she wanted to do. Especially
with the man who lived next door.

All she craved for was solitude, somewhere to hide
while her hurts healed, but the die was cast. She wasn't
going to get the chance to be just a stranger who nodded briefly during her comings and goings job-seeking
and then went in and closed the door.

But, as if to balance the scales, there were those two
lovely children and it would be a pleasure to babysit
them if ever Ryan felt he could trust her.

She'd also contacted the electricity people. She was
informed that they were on their way with a new meter

and were going to check all the primitive services and appliances in the house while they were there.

They arrived within minutes and as light began to appear in her darkness, in more ways than one, Melissa rolled up her sleeves and looked around her for what had to be her first task of the day. The guy who had just fixed the electricity meter decided it for her by pointing to an ancient but solid-looking gas fire and asking if she'd contacted the gas services yet as both the fire and an ancient cooker were gas powered.

She needed no second telling as having the fire working meant warmth and the cooker hot food, when she'd cleaned the grime off it and had the chance to shop.

The most pressing mission for Ryan, on his arrival at the hospital, was to start the search in earnest for the new registrar for their department.

The procedure with staff vacancies at the hospital was to advertise them internally first, but so far there had been no joy for the two consultants and the vacancy would soon be advertised locally

Today he had two clinics arranged for consultations, plus a slot in Theatre in the late afternoon. With all of that ahead of him he hadn't had time to check on how his new neighbour was coping at her house.

There'd been an electricity van outside and a plumber's vehicle pulling up alongside it as he'd driven past. He decided he owed her one more visit to check she was managing okay then he would step back and let her get on with her life while he got on with his.

The surgery he was committed to in the afternoon was minor compared to some of the operations he performed on unfortunate little ones and hopefully he would be home in time to have a quick word with Melissa before his special time with his children began.

As Ryan was preparing to put in an appearance at his first clinic of the day his assistant, Julian, appeared and commented breezily, 'Still no sign of a saviour in terms of over-booking, I see. Personnel need to pull their finger out and get us another doctor. I've got a list as long as my arm for today and I'm not used to it.'

Julian Tindall, with his dark attractiveness, was every woman's dream man, until they got to know him better!

Inclined to be lazy, but on the ball in an emergency, Julian was a paediatric consultant like himself and could go places if he stopped fooling around with every attractive woman he met and got his act together.

Ryan held the paediatric unit together with the kind of steadfastness that he applied to every aspect of his daily life, and if the nights spent without Beth by his side were long and lonely, only he knew that.

CHAPTER TWO

MELISSA'S SECOND DAY in Heatherdale was progressing and she was beginning to feel calmer. The neglected house was starting to come out of its murky cocoon, though not enough for her to rejoice totally. There was going to be mammoth amount of decorating and refurbishing to be done.

But the electricity was on, the plumber she'd asked to come had switched on the water and checked for leaks, and, joy of joys, the cleaners were hard at work, getting rid of the grime and mustiness of years.

Her clothes and the few belongings she had salvaged from the sale of the Cheshire house had arrived in the late afternoon. They included a couple of carpets, an expensive wardrobe and dressing table, a dining table and two easy chairs, but there was no kitchen equipment, which meant that for the time being she was going to have to manage with a solid-looking but unattractive gas cooker that was so old it would qualify as an antique.

Yet it had lit at the first attempt and as soon as the

cleaners had finished for the day with a promise to come back in the morning, she began to clean it, and was on her knees in front of it when a knock came on the door. She raised herself slowly upright.

With hair held back with a shoelace and dressed in an old pair of jeans and a much-washed jumper that the Cheshire set would never associate her with, she went slowly to answer the knock. He was there again, the Viking from next door, observing her with a reluctant sort of neighbourliness.

'I've called to see how you've fared today,' he said. 'I see that you've got lighting, but have you got heat and water?'

'Yes,' she replied, stepping back reluctantly for him to enter.

'I have light, and heat in the form of an old gas fire. A plumber has been to turn on the water. The cleaners have removed most of the dust and grime and are coming back in the morning to finish the job.'

'And I see that your belongings have arrived,' he said easily, as if she now had a house full of furniture instead of a few oddments. Unable to resist, he went on to ask, 'Do you have family who will be coming to join you?'

'No. Nothing like that,' she said in a low voice, without meeting his glance. She wished that he would go and leave her in peace. She'd seen the inside of his house and it was delightful, with décor and furniture that was just right for the age and design of the property, all obviously chosen with great care.

No doubt he was thinking that hers was going to lower the tone of the neighbourhood and for the first time since she'd arrived in Heatherdale the grim pride and determination that had helped her to stagger through recent months surfaced.

As if he sensed that she wanted him gone, Ryan moved towards the door but paused with his hand on the handle and said, 'I'm sure that you will like it here once you have made the house look how you want it to be.' He would have to be blind not to realise that she wasn't happy about coming to live in Heatherdale.

He almost asked if she would like to eat with them again but sensed the same reluctance as the night before. He bade her goodbye and, determined to put Melissa Redmond to the back of his mind, he went to join his daughters and the faithful Mollie, without whom he would be harassed full time.

'I saw you call at the house next door,' she said when he appeared. 'Is she all right? It has been all systems go in there today.'

'Yes, it would seem so,' he told her. 'I felt she was relieved that I didn't linger. I get a distinct feeling that Melissa Redmond wants to be left alone.'

'Give her time,' she said. 'The lass looked totally traumatised when we saw her last night. Something isn't right in her life. It stands out a mile, or she wouldn't have come here to live in a house that hasn't been touched for years. Don't forget the couple of times that you've seen her she won't have been at her best.'

'Yes, I suppose you're right,' he said absently, as

Rhianna and Martha came running down the stairs at that moment, and as he hugged them to him the stranger next door was forgotten in the pleasure of the moment.

When Ryan had gone, Melissa sank down onto the bottom step of the stairs. The cooker and its requirements temporarily forgotten, she gazed into space.

She wondered what Ryan did for a living. When she'd joined them for breakfast it had been plain to see that he was a loving father in the absence of a mother who wasn't around any more, yet he would have to earn a living somehow or other.

There was an air of authority about him that was noticeable and, much as she was not eager to be involved in the lives of those around her, she couldn't help wondering about him.

Still, there were more important priorities than getting to know the neighbours in this town, which would fit in a corner of Manchester. Such as turning her grandmother's house into a home and finding a job. Dared she intrude on the man next door once again by asking him for information about the famous hospital that she would love to be part of, and the local job centre in that order, so that tomorrow she would have a head start on the employment scene? No sooner had the thought occurred to her than she was acting on it.

Changing her working clothes for a stylish cashmere top, which belonged to happier days, and skinny jeans, Melissa was pressing his doorbell seconds later. When the door opened and he was framed there, looking not the least surprised, she said awkwardly, 'I wondered if you might be able to tell me anything about Heatherdale Hospital? Also, can you let me know where the job centre is? I'm going to go looking for employment tomorrow.'

'In that case, hadn't you better come in?'

She nodded awkwardly and stepped past him into the hall with its beautiful staircase, aware from the surprise in his glance that it was the first time he had seen her looking even the least bit attractive. As she waited for him to say something she felt herself reddening.

'Are you aware that Heatherdale Hospital is for children only?' he asked, breaking into the moment. 'If you feel that you need some sort of hospital treatment, you will have to go to Manchester.'

She was smiling. 'I need the information about the hospital because I would just die for the chance to work there.'

'Doing what?' he asked, with raised brows.

'I've got a degree in paediatrics. When I qualified in the summer I was offered a position at a big Manchester hospital and loved it, but that came to an end when my life fell apart. I had to resign because I intended to leave the area due to my family circumstances.'

So that was what she'd meant when she'd said she had a job making sick children well again. At the time Ryan had wondered if she was employed by some sort of charity, but it seemed she was much more hands on

than that, and incredibly he and Julian needed someone like her. Melissa Redmond might be heaven sent!

Obviously he'd never seen her in action. The offer
he was going to make her at this moment would be a
temporary one until he had her measure, and aware that
they were still standing in the hall as she had meant
it to be just a brief call on her part, he said, 'Come
through to the sitting room, while I make *my* contribution to this night of surprises.'

When they were seated with her eyes fixed on him
questioningly he said, 'How would you like to work
with me at Heatherdale Children's Hospital?'

'What?' she gasped. 'I don't understand.'

'I'm the paediatric consultant for the neurology
wards there and my assistant and I need another registrar to help with the workload. It would be on probationary terms at first but with the opportunity of
permanency for the right person. What do you say?
Do you want to give it a try?'

'Of course I do!' she breathed, her eyes shining. 'I
had no idea that was what you did for a living.'

'I don't mean to pry, Melissa, but can you tell me
something about what brought you to Heatherdale? I
need to know if it would have any effect on your work
and position at the hospital.'

She nodded mutely, took a deep breath. 'My father
died six months ago as a result of a road accident when
he'd had quite a lot of alcohol. From having a life of
luxury and pampering I became penniless because,

unbeknown to me, he'd accumulated huge gambling debts over the last couple of years.

'I was engaged to be married at the time and fully expected that my future husband would be there to support me as I dealt with bailiffs and demands for payment from those that my father owed money to, but I was mistaken.

'My fiancé couldn't break off the engagement fast enough, and once I'd paid all my father's debts, which meant selling the fabulous house we'd lived in, all I could think of was leaving the area and finding a bolt hole, somewhere to lick my wounds. The only answer to that was my grandmother's house, which is a far cry from the property I'd lived in before but is mine and isn't tainted. So there you have it, a sorry story worthy of a reality TV show.'

'Thanks for telling me,' Ryan said. 'We all have our nightmares to face at one time or another and you have certainly faced up to yours. Can you come to the hospital some time tomorrow and I'll show you round and introduce you to people, including Personnel, who will need you to fill out endless forms.'

'Yes, of course,' she breathed. 'Thank you for giving me the opportunity to get back into paediatrics. I love working with children and hope to have some of my own one day.'

He nodded as the memory of Rhianna and Martha's approval of their breakfast guest resurfaced. The stranger who had come to Heatherdale in the dark of a winter night would make some child a loving mother one day in every sense of the word, he imagined, just as Beth had been to their children.

'What time do you want me to come to the hospital?' she asked.

'Some time in the afternoon when my clinics are over and I'm not in Theatre, around three—unless you have something else planned at that time?'

'No, I haven't,' she told him firmly.

She'd intended spending the afternoon looking for a washing machine that would fit in with her budget but that could wait, everything could wait. He was offering her the chance to be back where she wanted to be, and if Ryan Ferguson was willing to take a chance on her she was not going to disappoint him.

Later that night, for the first time in months sleep came like a healing balm.

A wintry sun was shining overhead as Melissa drove to the famous children's hospital the next afternoon, and although her mind was full of what lay ahead she couldn't help but notice the beautiful architecture of some of the buildings she was passing.

Maybe the market town of Heatherdale wasn't going to be as dreary as she had expected it to be. Life was beginning to feel worth living again.

Walking away from her parked car, she looked around her. The hospital was another apparently ageless building, built from the beautiful local stone that seemed to be everywhere she looked. She hoped that its interior would not lack the trappings of the latest in modern medicine for the sake of its young patients.

There was no cause to be concerned about that. The inside was bright, cheerful and immaculate, with sunshine colours on the walls and lots of pictures of things that children would like.

As she followed the directions to the neuro wards Melissa's heart was beating faster. She was on home ground, within reach of being back on the job she loved once again.

She found Ryan at the bedside of a small girl, who had been brought in by an ambulance with sirens wailing, with what might be meningitis. It was a road he'd been down more times than he could count and it was never any less horrendous to have to tell a family that one of their little ones had succumbed to the dreadful illness.

There was a fellow doctor standing beside him, but his presence barely registered. Melissa's glance was fixed on the man who in a short space of time had brought some zest into her life. Not only had Ryan taken her in out of the cold that first night but he was going to be the means of finding her employment in the very place where she wanted to be.

He glanced up then, saw her standing in the doorway, and sent his assistant over to suggest that she join them as an observer of the emergency. With her adrenaline quickening, she was beside him in a flash.

'It seemed that the child had become very drowsy during the lunch hour. It had been then that her parents had noticed the tell-tale rash and it had become panic stations. While the ambulance had been speeding to the hospital the little girl had lapsed into unconsciousness.'

Ryan turned to the anxious couple at the other side of the bed and began to explain what would happen to their daughter next—blood tests and a lumbar puncture to test for bacterial meningitis.

When the parents and their sick little one had been taken with all speed for the tests, Ryan's colleague asked. 'So, are you going to introduce me, Ryan?'

'Yes, of course,' he said. 'Julian, meet my new neighbour, Melissa Redmond, recently employed in paediatrics in the Manchester area and now about to join us here on a probationary basis with a view to a permanent position. Melissa, this is Julian Tindall.'

Ryan noticed that she was looking a different person altogether today, dressed in smart clothes and with her hair and make-up perfect. She was quite beautiful in a restrained sort of way.

As Melissa shook hands with Julian she was aware of him sizing her up and immediately had him pegged as an attractive, dark-eyed flirt.

'So when do you want to start?' Ryan asked, 'To-morrow perhaps?'

'Er, yes, if that's all right with you.'

'Certainly, if you're available,' he replied.

She had never felt more 'available' in her life. He knew she was out on a limb here in Heatherdale, that apart from getting her house in order there was no one who cared a jot about her. Why wait to begin this job of a lifetime?

Melissa wished that there was someone to share her good news with, but the days were gone when she'd had a loving father, an attentive fiancé, and lots of friends to communicate with.

Her glance rested briefly on the house next door where she'd been welcomed into the home of a stranger and had been reluctant to accept his hospitality on a dark and lonely night. Ryan Ferguson must have thought her some sort of ungracious oddball.

The lights were on, which was not surprising as his children would be home from school by now and being looked after by his housekeeper. Melissa wondered again what had happened to their mother.

Whatever it was, the two of them had seemed happy enough until they'd discovered she was coming to live next door. Then had come the protest about it being haunted and she'd tried not to smile at their childish imaginings.

As afternoon turned into evening she saw there was no car outside so obviously Ryan wasn't home yet, and as she began to prepare a snack sort of meal, which was becoming the norm since life had become so drab and disillusioning, she hugged herself at the thought of tomorrow.

Ryan had phoned home to tell Mollie he would be late due to a seriously ill child with bacterial meningitis that he wanted to try to get stabilised before he left her in the care of the night staff.

It wasn't the first time he'd been late home because of his job and it wouldn't be the last, and on such occasions he was very grateful for Mollie's presence in their lives. She lived alone just down the road from them, having lost her husband from heart failure some years previously and was happy to be of use to him and his children to such an extent.

The girls were in bed by the time he arrived and after a brief chat and a cuddle he left them sleepy and contented to go downstairs to have the meal that Mollie had kept warm for him.

She wished that his life was less stressful, but knew it had been his choice to parent single-handedly after his wife's death. She admired him for the way he cared for his children. Yet she couldn't help wishing that someone would come along who would make Ryan realise what he was missing, that Beth would not have wanted him to be alone for the rest of his life, always involved with work or family when it came to the social life of the town and its hospital.

'I've found a new registrar to lighten our load at the hospital,' he told her as she placed the food in front of him.

'That's good!' she exclaimed. 'Another man, is it?'

'No, it's a woman. Actually, someone you know.'

'That I know?'

'Yes, it's Melissa from next door. She has a degree

in paediatrics and she joins us tomorrow. What do you think of that?'

'I'm amazed, but what a good thing for both of you that she has found employment so quickly and that your stresses will be lighter. It's as if her coming to live in Heatherdale was meant to be.'

Ryan smiled. 'Don't get too carried away, Mollie. I only found out about her qualifications last night and offered her the job on condition that she fits the bill, so it will be probationary to begin with.'

'Yes, of course,' Mollie agreed, thankful that something was going right for him for once.

The blood tests and lumbar puncture had shown that little Georgia had indeed got bacterial meningitis and he'd explained to her distraught parents that she was going to be given large doses of antibiotics that he'd arranged for her to have intravenously in the hope of preventing the dreaded illness increasing its hold on her.

When he'd eventually left the hospital it had been with the determination to ring the ward later for a report on her progress as the next few hours would be crucial.

The answer was what he'd hoped for when he did. His small patient was regaining consciousness and her horrendously high temperature was coming down, so with Mollie having returned home and Rhianna and Martha asleep, Ryan decided to spend the rest of the evening with a medical journal that had been languishing on the back seat of his car for a few days.

When he went out to get it he saw that the house next door was in darkness and he observed it thoughtfully. What was the bet that Melissa was having an early night so that she would be bright-eyed and bushy-tailed tomorrow?

He supposed it could be said that it hadn't been a good idea to offer her a job working with him most of the time, but discovering that she was in paediatrics had been too good a chance to miss in his busy working life. He went back into the house in a thoughtful mood and with the feeling that maybe he needed to cool it where she was concerned.

It was an eight o'clock start for day staff on the wards and the next morning Melissa watched as Ryan kissed his children goodbye with Mollie in attendance, and drove off.

As the taillights of his car disappeared she followed him at a distance, having no wish to be on the last minute on her first day at the hospital.

Today could or could not be the beginning of a new life. A life on a lower level than before maybe, when the envious had called her 'golden girl', but at least she would have some dignity, wouldn't be an object of pity or sly smirks.

In the short time that she'd been in the house she had been aware that something strange was happening. The children next door had said it was haunted and she wasn't going to go along with *that*, but one thing she did feel was that the grandmother she had never really known was somewhere near, content that the one person she had always wanted to live in her house had arrived.

Miserable and lonely she may be, but she was there in the house that had been bequeathed to her all those years ago because the old lady had foreseen what the future might hold for her pleasure-loving son's child. Today Melissa was about to take the first step towards becoming a working member of the community.

CHAPTER THREE

RYAN HAD SEEN Melissa arrive from the window of his office, which overlooked the car park. She was so different from the woman he had been confronted with just a couple of nights ago, it was unbelievable. Her hair, her clothes, the newfound calm had altered her totally.

She was still the stranger who had erupted into his life from nowhere but she was no longer nondescript. Yesterday, when she'd come to the hospital to have a look round and meet Julian and any of the nurses who were present, he'd thought that she was beautiful and still did. Not in a voluptuous sort of way but fine-boned and slender.

Still, there was the promise he had made to himself to cool it with regard to Melissa Redmond. The absence of a woman in his life in the true sense meant that never again would there be the agony of loss such as he'd suffered when he'd lost Beth.

With that in mind he wished Melissa a cool good

morning when they met at the entrance to the wards and suggested that she find herself a white hospital coat.

'I've brought one with me from my last job,' she told him, and wondered who had rubbed Ryan up the wrong way so early in the day.

It wasn't likely to be Julian as so far there was no sign of him having arrived, though on the other hand that might be the reason for Ryan's abrupt manner. Whatever it was, she was determined that nothing was going to blight this day of all days.

Julian came strolling down the corridor towards them at that moment and she flashed him a smile, and after putting on the white hospital coat followed them into the ward.

'I'd like you to do the ward rounds with Julian today,' Ryan told her. 'Watch and learn and you'll soon get the hang of things. Little Georgia is in one of the side wards where she is making a good recovery, and her parents are with her most of the time.

'We also have a ten-year-old boy with us who is a new admission. He suffered a head injury when he fell off his bike. It's quite serious, but at the moment does not require surgery.'

Then Ryan looked straight at Melissa.

'Some time this afternoon I'd like a brief word with you. In the meantime, when the two of you have finished rounds, Julian will direct you to Personnel so that you can get the processing of a new employee over and done with.'

'Yes, fine,' she said, having decided that she was

being given the hint that being neighbours didn't mean any special treatment. As if she would expect anything of that kind.

Maybe it was Ryan's way of letting her see that his efforts on her behalf since arriving in Heatherdale were now at an end, and if that *was* the case it would have no effect on the deep gratitude she felt for the kindness he had shown her.

'I wonder what's upset the boss?' Julian mused when Ryan had gone. 'He was rather abrupt. Ryan needs some light relief in his life. He's all work and no play.'

Melissa didn't comment. There was no way she would discuss Ryan with Julian, who, from the sound of it, hadn't a care in the world.

Back in his office Ryan reminded himself that from now on he would be able to relax at the thought of Melissa in the house next door with her few belongings. If she could turn up looking like she had the last two days he need not concern himself about her any more, and that being so he would find it easier to have a good working relationship with her instead of behaving like he just had.

Ryan's crustiness forgotten, Melissa enjoyed every moment of her first morning on the wards with Julian. She would have much preferred it to be with 'the boss', as his laid-back assistant called him, but it was sufficient that she was working in a hospital once more. She read the records of every young patient's treatment and progress thoroughly when they stopped by their beds and asked Julian questions if she wasn't clear about anything.

That afternoon Ryan requested her presence for the brief chat that he'd mentioned earlier in the day, and she went to his office expecting a repeat of the brisk instructions of the morning. She was surprised to see him smiling. She was unaware that he had decided that now there was no longer any need of his help as far as she was concerned, he could relax and return to what life had been like before she'd appeared in it.

'I just wanted to ask how your first day is going,' he said. 'I know how much you wanted to be back in paediatrics.'

'Fantastic,' she told him, 'The chance to work here is the best thing that has happened to me in years and it is all due to you.' She didn't want to give him the wrong impression.

'I'll be fine from now on, Ryan, with the house that I'm going to make as delightful as yours one day, and working here with Julian and yourself, I'm back to the self-reliant person I used to be.'

Still on a high on her way home, she stopped to collect colour charts for paints and some wallpaper samples and once she'd eaten she sat considering them thoughtfully. Renovating the house that was now her home would have to be carefully budgeted, but it also had to be right for the property.

She'd seen the interior design of the house next door and had been aware of how right it was for that kind of house, and though having no wish to copy it, she felt that she needed to keep to a similar kind of décor.

The first room to be transformed was going to be the sitting room so she decided on a heavily embossed wallpaper of red and gold to match the big ornate fireplace that, along with large leaded windows, dominated the room. She sat back in the chair and imagined what it would look like and excitement spiralled at the thought.

Her second day at the hospital felt less strange now she'd adjusted to the fact that Ryan was going to be around most of the time while she was working as well as living next door, but as it was she saw little of him.

His car was there so he was around somewhere, but apart from a glimpse of him at the end of the corridor, talking sombrely to the parents of a patient, he never appeared, and when she queried his absence Julian explained that he had meetings scheduled all day with the hospital hierarchy. He added that she couldn't have joined them at a better time.

On her way home that evening she ventured into the main shopping area of Heatherdale and bought a long ladder that would reach way up towards the ceiling, a large can of white emulsion paint, and the paper that she had chosen for the walls, along with the paste that would be needed to fix it.

An obliging shopkeeper offered to drop off her purchases on his way home after closing the place and he delivered them shortly after she arrived at the house.

She'd never done any decorating before, but of late that had applied to a lot of things that she'd had to face up to, and as soon as she'd had her usual scrappy meal Melissa put on the old clothes she'd worn on the day of moving in and began to climb the ladder with the can of emulsion paint and the roller she was going to use while she painted the ceiling.

Ryan had arrived home shortly after Melissa and as he'd pulled up in front of their two houses had observed the delivery of the decorating materials and the stepladder, and been amazed at the size of it. He'd sighed. What was she up to now? Whatever it might be, he wasn't going to get involved, at least not until he'd eaten the meal that Mollie had prepared for him and the children.

Melissa was getting the hang of it. The roller went back and forth across the age-old ceiling with her standing firmly on her lofty perch. As long as she didn't look down, she would be fine.

At that moment the doorbell rang and as the heavy oak door was on the latch it swung open. As she turned quickly to see who was there, the stepladder swung backwards and sent her flying through the air with a terrified scream.

Ryan caught her just before she hit the floor, absorbing the impact of her fall.

'I am so sorry to be such a nuisance.' She gasped.

He was still holding her close and made no reply,

just kept looking down at her. It was the first time he'd held a woman like this since he'd lost Beth and it was gut-wrenching. He'd always known it would be and had made sure that it never happened for his sanity's sake, but with Melissa it was as if he just couldn't avoid her—she was everywhere he turned and he didn't want it to be like that.

Putting her carefully back onto her feet, he said abruptly, 'Whatever possessed you to try something as dangerous as painting this high ceiling? You should have hired a decorator.'

'It would be too expensive,' she replied, wishing those moments in his arms had affected him as much as they'd affected her. She'd felt safe and protected as he'd held her close and it seemed like a lifetime since she'd last had those sorts of feelings.

But she'd sensed tension in him as he'd held her in his arms, a reluctance to have her in such close contact, and her morale had been low enough of late without another putdown, in more ways than one.

'That's because you're new to the area. I know someone who would do this place up for you at a very reasonable rate and make an excellent job of it. Why don't you let me give him a buzz and ask him to come round to give you a quote? You wouldn't be under any obligation.'

'Er, yes, all right,' she agreed reluctantly, 'and thank you on both counts, for catching me and breaking my fall, *and* for offering to put me in touch with someone I can trust to do some decorating. I've had cause to discover recently that people I thought I could trust were not like that at all, far from it. Still, that's in the past. For now I suppose I'd better start cleaning up.'

'I guess so,' he agreed, 'and I'd better get back to my place. Mollie will be getting ready to go home and my children will be waiting to play their favourite game, "Hospitals". They've both got a nurse's uniform.'

He was smiling at the thought and went on to amaze himself by saying, 'Their mother was a midwife. She went out on a late-night call in the middle of a raging storm to supervise an imminent birth, and a tree that was rotten at the roots fell across the car. She didn't survive the injuries it caused.'

'Oh! How awful!' she breathed. 'You must miss her very much.'

'Yes,' he said flatly. 'I do. More than words can say. The newborn was a girl and they called her Beth after the midwife who had been true to her calling in spite of a horrendous storm.'

On that bombshell, Ryan wished Melissa a brief goodnight, and unable to believe that he had actually talked about the worst time of his life to a stranger of all people, he went back to where his motherless children were waiting for him.

When he'd gone Melissa began to clean up the mess but her mind wasn't on it. She had her answer now to the questions about the loss of his wife.

But surely Ryan wasn't intending to spend the rest of his life alone and loveless? Yet wasn't she intending to do something similar? To have been cast aside because her cash value had dropped suddenly had made her realise what a farce her engagement had been, had made her see how gullible and trusting she'd been.

She shuddered every time she thought that someone as shallow as David Lowson could have been the father of any children she might have had. What a contrast between him and the man next door who had put himself out of circulation for the sake of his children, *and in memory of the woman he had loved.*

She really would have to stop being such an intrusion in his life. It wasn't intentional, no one needed to be solitary more than she did, having lost her faith in love and friendship. If Ryan was regretting having got involved with her again about the decorating and on second thoughts decided to let it lapse, she would understand.

When the bell rang a second time an hour later Melissa was expecting it to be Ryan, fobbing her off with an excuse about being unable to find her a decorator.

It was not so. A man in his sixties stood on the doorstep, and as she eyed him questioningly he said, 'Ryan has just phoned to say that you have some decorating that you want doing.'

'Er, yes, I have,' she told him. 'Do come in. I've just moved in and the whole place has been neglected. I tried to paint the ceiling and fell off the ladder.'

'I'm not surprised,' he commented. 'These are very high ceilings.

'Tell me what you want done and I'll call back tomorrow with an estimate. If you agree to it I'll start right away. I wonder if you realise how lucky you are to be the owner of a town house in a place like Heatherdale?'

'I'm afraid I haven't seen it in that light so far,' she told him wryly.

'You will' was the reply. 'We have a well that supplies our very own spa water all the time and is available to all comers, and the most beautiful gardens and historical buildings.'

He held out a capable-looking hand for her to shake and said, 'The name is Smethurst. I'll be round tomorrow with a price if you'll tell me what you want doing. Is it just this sitting room, or the whole place?'

'Just this room to begin with,' she told him, 'but I'm sure that by the time you've done it I will be wanting you to do more.'

'Fair enough,' he agreed. 'See you tomorrow, then,' and went striding off into the dark winter night.

When he'd gone she felt ashamed for presuming that Ryan would have wanted to back out of his offer to find her a decorator, and at the risk of making a further nuisance of herself she went next door to thank him for his prompt attention to her needs.

The children were asleep and Ryan had just settled down to what was going to be his first free time of the day when the doorbell rang. He sighed and, getting to his feet, turned the television down low and went to answer it.

When he saw Melissa standing there his first thought

was that it was getting to be too much of a habit, them toing and froing between each other's houses. He'd done what he'd said he would do and phoned Jack Smethurst. What more did she want from him?

'Hello again,' he said observing her unsmilingly. 'What can I do for you this time? I hope you haven't been up the ladder again. I did tell you I would phone the decorator.'

'Yes, I know you did,' she replied with a sinking feeling that she should have waited until morning to express her thanks. 'That's why I'm here. He has been and—'

'What? Already!' he exclaimed. Regretting his churlishness, he added, 'Do come in out of the cold.'

She shook her head. The night *was* cold, but his greeting had been colder. 'No, thank you. I don't want to disturb you any further. Mr Smethurst is letting me have an estimate tomorrow and I just wanted to thank you for putting me in touch with him.'

As she turned to go she gave a gasp of pain and he stepped towards her. 'What's wrong?'

'It's nothing,' she told him hurriedly. 'Just a pulled neck muscle from when I fell off the ladder. I'll take a painkiller when I get in. Goodnight, Ryan.' And before he could reply she was gone, hurrying towards her own front door in the dark night and wishing that she'd stayed put instead of making a nuisance of herself again.

When Melissa had gone, Ryan sat deep in thought with the memory of the mixture of emotions that had gripped him when he'd held her in his arms. There had been shock at the suddenness of it, relief that he'd been able to break her fall, and uppermost there had been a combined feeling of loss and longing that had broken down the barriers of the celibate life that he had chosen for himself.

Once back in his own house he had calmed down, telling himself that the episode had just been a one off, it could have happened with anyone, and would not be referred to tomorrow as far as he was concerned.

But when he'd answered the ring on the doorbell it had seemed that the day was not yet over where he and Melissa Redmond were concerned and he'd been offhand and unwelcoming, afraid to become too closely involved in her life.

The next morning Ryan waited beside his car until Melissa appeared. He asked if she was experiencing any after-effects of the fall, knowing that it must have jarred every bone in her body.

Dredging up a smile, she told him, 'Just one or two minor aches and pains, that's all.'

She *was* experiencing after-effects but they were mental rather than physical and had kept her awake most of the night, so she was not in the mood to start mellowing at the sight of him. She'd be polite, yes, he was her boss who had saved her from what could have been serious injuries, but afterwards he had let her see that enough was enough.

Ryan changed the subject. 'I've got some catching

up to do today. Meetings are a bind when there is work to be done and yesterday's seemed to drag on for ever. Julian reports that you are a natural on the job, manna from heaven, so that's good.'

He didn't say any more, just jumped into his car and drove off, with her following once again. She didn't know what to make of Ryan's mood swings but, then, she was unaware that he had also slept fitfully with the memory of her in his arms sweet torment.

As the long hours of the night had dragged by Melissa had told herself that his manner when she'd gone to thank him for sorting out a decorator would have told even the most unobservant of people that he felt he was seeing too much of her, that she was forever at his elbow.

But the realisation had been there that as far as she was concerned it was a case of *her* not seeing enough of *him*. That was the real reason for her seeking him out again, and having those sorts of feelings for him was the last thing she wanted to happen. Since her father's death her hurts had been many and she had no wish to add to them. Being rejected by one man was enough to be going on with.

When Melissa arrived home that evening the estimate from the decorator was on the doormat and she could have wept with relief at the amount he was asking for decorating the sitting room. She phoned him immediately to tell him to go ahead as soon as possible and did a little dance around the room in question when she'd made the call.

'I'll be round in the morning,' Jack Smethurst had said. 'Mollie next door will let me in if you give her a key.' And that was that. Ryan had turned one of her most urgent needs into something simple and it would be difficult not to do a repeat of last night's display of gratitude.

But she had got the message loud and clear from his manner on that occasion, that just because he'd done her a good turn he didn't want her to disturb him further.

Mollie had gone. Ryan and the children had finished their evening meal and after stacking the dishwasher he did what he'd been wanting to do ever since arriving home. He rang Jack Smethurst to enquire if Melissa had accepted his estimate.

'She has indeed' was the reply. 'I'll be starting in the morning. I've asked the young lady to leave a key with Mollie. Hope you don't mind.'

'No, not at all,' Ryan told him. When Melissa dropped the key in later Ryan was determined that he wouldn't be so surly when he opened the door to her this time.

But it was eleven o'clock and she still hadn't been with the key. He'd been listening for her to ring the doorbell all evening and when he went into the hall to see if her lights were still on he saw the key on the mat with a note beside it to say that she hoped he wouldn't mind passing the key on to Mollie as Mr Smethurst had assured her that it would be all right.

He groaned. The night before he'd made sure that Melissa had got the message that he wasn't to be contacted out of working hours, and she hadn't forgotten.

Of course Mollie would give the decorator the key when he came. Jack Smethurst and Mollie were dating. If they decided to tie the knot at some future date he might have to find himself another housekeeper, but he had learned to live one day at a time since he'd lost Beth. His children and the job were his lifelines, as he was theirs, and any further than that he wasn't going to contemplate.

As he went slowly up to bed the thought came that Christmas would soon begin to spread its mantle over the ancient market town that was so dear to his heart. He wondered what his new neighbour would have planned for that. She might surprise him and have a house full of relatives turn up.

It would be his third one without Beth and an ordeal to be got through, just as the two previous ones had been, but he would cope for Rhianna and Martha's sakes.

The first sign of the coming festivities would be in a couple of weeks' time when the town's brass band would play a selection of carols outside the old pump room.

There would be mulled wine and mince pies on offer with presents for the children from a bran tub, and the residents of Heatherdale and folk from far and wide would be there, keeping up the traditions of a bygone age.

But before that there would be what there always was, young lives needing a gift of another kind, that of a healthy body, and Ryan was forever thankful that he could help towards that end in his clinic, on the wards and in the operating theatre.

As he pulled back the curtains to let the light of a winter moon into his bedroom and lay back against the pillows Ryan wondered just how close Melissa was to him at the other side of the wall.

The next morning Ryan had already left when Melissa sallied forth. She'd been waved off by Mollie and the children, who were still in their nightdresses at that early hour.

It wasn't until she and Ryan met on the wards that he had a chance to speak to Melissa, and his first words were, 'Good news about the decorating. I've given Mollie your key to pass on to Jack.'

'Yes, I can't wait to see it,' she said wistfully, with a vision of the furnishings in the house she'd had to sell coming to mind, but why was Ryan suddenly so chatty? Could it be that he had decided that there was no cause for unease, that she posed no threat to his organised existence?

When Rhianna and Martha had waved her off that morning she had felt a lump come up in her throat. Ryan may have lost his wife but he still had his children to cherish, safe and happy, while she had no one.

As if to emphasise that fact, Julian had caught her up in the car park and looking around him had said, 'I see that the boss is here before us, needless to say. He's always first on the job, as if he hasn't a moment to spare.'

'If you mean Dr Ferguson, maybe he hasn't,' she'd said dryly. 'I think he's amazing.'

'So do a lot of other women,' he'd told her, 'but sooner or later they have to accept that he is a one-woman man, even though the woman in question isn't around any more. If he ever decided to get married again, they would be queuing up.'

'Really!' she'd commented, and had left it at that. There was no way she was going to discuss with Julian the man who had been her saviour at one of the darkest times of her life.

After their brief chat about the decorating the day began satisfactorily from a medical point of view. Ryan dished out instructions. 'We have two clinics today, Melissa. I'm taking one and Julian the other. I want you to sit in at mine as joining me whenever you can will be a big part of your duties until you are ready to take a clinic of your own.'

She was smiling. The job, the wonderful job, was like balm to her soul. Even if Ryan never ever did her another good turn she would bless him for ever for this chance to use the skills that she'd had to put to one side.

As adults with children appeared before them, one lot after another, he turned to her frequently and asked her advice, explaining to them that she was a doctor from a Manchester hospital who they were pleased to have as a new member of staff at Heatherdale.

The courtesy of his introduction brought the sting of tears after dealing with debt collectors and bailiffs for months, with the added pain of missing friends and an ex-fiancé.

When the clinic was over he said briskly, 'Well done. You are going to be a big help to me. When you've had a break go back on the wards with Julian for a late-morning round.' When Melissa didn't immediately answer he asked, 'Are you all right?'

'Yes,' she breathed. 'Oh, yes!'

She was, from a job point of view, but Julian's comments about Ryan earlier had taken her into uncharted territory, and she knew that of all things she must be careful where he was concerned. The last thing she would want was to become one of the hopefuls waiting in the wings.

Ryan was very pleased. It wouldn't be long before Melissa was taking a clinic of her own. Maybe an extra doctor on the unit would give him more time with the children, as well as it being the answer to some of her problems. Further than that he was not going to think. A good relationship on the unit was enough to be going on with and as he hadn't given her any cause to think otherwise it should work all right.

CHAPTER FOUR

THE DECORATING OF the sitting room was finished and Melissa was delighted with it, so much so that when she arrived home and saw it on the evening of the third day of the transformation she had to restrain herself from going to the house next door to invite Ryan and his children to come and see it.

When she'd been on the point of leaving for the hospital that morning, Jack Smethurst had asked, 'Do I take it that the roll of pale gold carpet is for in here?'

'Yes,' she'd told him, and had wondered if Ryan was also acquainted with a carpet fitter. He'd found her a decorator so maybe he was.

It was one of the two lengths of carpet that the buyers of the Cheshire house hadn't insisted be included in the sale and she'd chosen the red-and-gold wallpaper with it in mind.

And now she saw that she needn't have concerned herself about the fitting of it as the carpet had been laid and was the perfect finishing touch to the room. She could have wept with thankfulness.

On observing that no charge had been made for it

on the account that had been left for her, she vowed that the first thing she would do when the decorator came for payment would be to ask how much she owed him for the extra work.

What Melissa couldn't know was that the night before Ryan had said to Jack Smethurst, 'I saw the wallpaper that time when Melissa fell off the ladder and presume that the gold carpet is to go with it. If she says that it is, will you fit it and let me have the bill? And don't tell Mollie or she'll be shopping around for a wedding outfit. Although she never puts it into words, I know she worries about my solitary state.'

Jack had laughed. 'She's already looking for an outfit but it's not for your wedding, it's for ours, so be warned, but don't worry. She loves the three of you too much to stay away from you for long, and, yes, I'll see to the carpet, but tell me, why are you doing this? You hardly know the woman.'

'I met Melissa on the night she came to live in Heatherdale and she was in a dreadful state. The house was filthy and she'd been let down by the cleaners, but it wasn't just that. I felt that something had happened to her beyond bearing. She was like a lost soul and I can't forget it, even though she is so different now, employed at the hospital, making her house fit to live in, and doesn't seem so alone as she did then.

'But there is still something about her that worries me, that's why I want her to have the pleasure of seeing the carpet fitted and the room finished when she comes home tomorrow. So do we have a deal? And don't forget, Jack, not a word to Melissa about it...ever.'

'Yes, if you say so' had been the reply.

It was no use, Melissa decided. Whether Ryan approved or not, she just had to go and tell him how thrilled she was to have at least one room fit to live in. Surely he wouldn't object to what he usually saw as an intrusion because he was the one who had caught her when she'd fallen off the ladder and found her a decorator.

His car was outside so he was home, but she was going to restrain herself until he and his family had finished their evening meal. It wouldn't be fair to butt in before that and so she made herself a sandwich and spent the next half-hour gazing rapturously around her.

She was about to venture forth when the phone rang and she was spared having to seek him out.

'I hope you don't mind me ringing,' he said, 'If you remember, I asked for your phone number when you started at the hospital in case I had to get in touch with you regarding an emergency of some kind on our patch.'

'No, not at all,' she replied, relieved that it was Ryan's turn to cross the privacy line. 'What can I do for you?'

'You can tell me how the room looks. Are you happy with it?'

'Over the moon,' she told him with a lift to her voice. 'And guess what, Ryan? Your decorator friend has fitted the carpet for me and it looks dreamy.'

He was smiling and carried away by her delight. 'So is it all right if I bring a bottle of champagne to celebrate the occasion and the girls and I come to admire the transformation?'

'Yes, of course,' she said eagerly, and went on to tell him laughingly, 'Just as long as Rhianna and Martha won't be expecting to see a ghost. The only person here who is a shadow of their former self is me!'

When they arrived shortly afterwards Ryan was carrying the champagne and his daughters were on either side of him. He saw that Melissa was wrapped around with delight and hoped she would not discover his part in the fitting of the carpet.

While he was thinking those sorts of thoughts Melissa had been into the kitchen and had come back with the champagne in two flutes out of boxes of oddments that had survived the removal, and with glasses of fruit juice for the children.

Ryan raised his glass. 'So, now that you have an elegant sitting room, does it mean that you are going to stay here in Heatherdale and make the rest of the house as attractive as this room?'

'Yes,' she said. 'The place is growing on me. When I went into the centre the other day I was entranced by the beauty of the architecture and the pump room with the well beside it forever providing the famous spa waters. I think I might get to like Heatherdale. I am already over the moon with its hospital, and in any case I can't afford to buy or even rent another property elsewhere.'

The conversation was about to take an awkward turn. Martha had come to stand by her side and looking up at her said, 'Do you know any mummies? When you came to breakfast you said that *you* weren't a mummy, but we thought you might know where there is one.'

Although her glance was fixed on the small questioner, Melissa could feel Ryan's tension so keenly it was as if he was glued to her side, and she said with great gentleness, 'I'm afraid I don't, Martha, but you have got a lovely daddy, haven't you?'

'Yes,' Rhianna chipped in, 'but lots of our friends have a mummy as well as a daddy.'

Ryan was cringing. 'That is enough from both of you. We came here to look at Melissa's house, not to be impolite and nosey.'

'It's all right,' she assured him. 'I understand.' And to take the sting out of what he'd said to them, she went on, 'They are lovely children, Ryan, a credit to you.'

He was not to be humoured. 'I'm not looking for "credit" and now I think we shall go. Say goodnight to Melissa,' he told his daughters and as they wished her a subdued farewell, unable to help herself, she bent and kissed them both, holding them close just for a second.

In return they clung to her and when she looked up she saw pain in Ryan's expression and was immediately sorry for causing a situation that would have no joy in it for him. Ryan marched to the door, opened it, and waited for Rhianna and Martha to leave her side.

When they'd stepped out on to the drive he said in a low voice that was for her ears only, 'It would seem that I am not very successful with regard to my children's contentment, although it is only since they met you that this kind of thing has kept cropping up.'

'I'm sorry,' she said. 'I meant no harm, Ryan. They're both so appealing I couldn't resist holding them close for a moment.'

He nodded. 'I suppose that's fair enough.' And taking them by the hand he went with a brief goodbye.

When Rhianna and Martha were asleep he stood looking down at them with the feeling that he'd behaved like a complete moron by objecting to a moment's affection for them from Melissa.

Martha had never fretted about not having Beth around before. He doubted that her fixation with the subject was because Melissa reminded her of her mother as she was not like her in any way. Maybe she sensed something about her that she and Rhianna needed, something that he couldn't see but which the eyes of a child saw, and he was just going to have to live with the disruption in their lives that it was causing until it had passed. He'd felt sick inside as he'd watched them lift up their faces to be kissed. His heart broke for them all.

They left their respective houses the next morning with the same thought in mind. Whatever had been in their minds the night before, today they both had jobs to do. His far more important than hers, and as tomorrow was Saturday Melissa hoped that the weekend would give them the chance to avoid any further uncomfortable meetings.

The trouble was that Ryan knew only the brief details of her past that she'd told him on the day when she'd first gone to the hospital. Was it any wonder he was wary of his children getting too close to a virtual stranger?

Thankfully their positions at the hospital had an impersonal approach that gave them some degree of separation otherwise it could be awkward, to say the least.

Having made a good recovery from the meningitis, young Georgia was due to go home and, as was sometimes the case, her grateful parents had brought a bottle of something for the doctor who had saved her life and chocolates for the nurses. As they were ready to leave, Georgia's father said to Melissa, 'We are having a party next Saturday to celebrate having our little daughter back with us and would like Dr Ferguson to be there, but he tells us that he has other commitments. Can you not persuade him to change his mind?'

As if! she thought. She was the last person Ryan would take note of, and in any case he was certain to have something planned with Rhianna and Martha, so she smiled and said that she had no authority over him.

She didn't see Ryan again during the rest of the morning. He and Julian were both taking clinics and she'd been left to do the rounds while they were absent.

When she was taking a short lunch break in the staff

restaurant Julian appeared and for once his expression was grave. 'What's wrong?' she questioned.

'Two young lads and their respective parents were at the clinic this morning,' he informed her, 'and both of the youngsters have been diagnosed with muscular dystrophy, which, as you know, is caused by a faulty inherited gene from somewhere back in their families. Ryan had the ghastly job of telling them.'

'Not telling the children surely?' she questioned.

'No, of course not,' Julian replied. 'Just the parents. It is at their discretion what they tell the youngsters.'

'There have been some huge steps forward with regard to muscular dystrophy over the years,' she reminded him. 'Diagnosis and treatment have advanced a great deal.'

'You seem to be well informed,' a voice said from behind her, and Ryan was there, the golden Viking who was just as fierce as men of old when it came to protecting those who belonged to him.

She didn't deny it. 'Yes, I am. I've been on a course about the illness.'

Julian had been to the counter and was coming back with sandwiches and coffee for the two of them. Having no wish to intrude into their lunch break, Melissa got to her feet and left them to it.

The rest of the day passed uneventfully and so did the evening, with the only interruption the arrival of the decorator to enquire if she was satisfied with the room now that it was finished.

'It's perfect,' she told him, 'and I can't thank you enough for fitting the carpet. Do you want to add it on to the original account, or give me a separate one? Either way will be fine, but I would like to pay for all the work that you've done while you're here.'

'The fitting of the carpet is included in the first fig- ure I quoted,' Jack Smethurst said awkwardly, with the memory clear of Ryan's stipulation that Melissa must not know about his being involved in it.

'But you didn't know then that I was going to have it put down in the sitting room,' she persisted.

'I suppose I guessed,' he replied, and thought that Ryan's concern for her was complicating what should be a simple payment for a job well done.

Still unconvinced, Melissa wrote out a cheque for the original quote and when he'd gone decided that if she asked him to do any more work for her she would insist at the time of asking that he give her a separate price for the laying of any carpets, or carpet, as she'd only brought the two pieces with her.

As it was, she could only feel that Ryan had done her a really good turn by recommending Mollie's man friend to do the job, and when he had gone she sat un- moving with the thought of the coming weekend on her own bringing no joy.

She'd seen the signs of Christmastime appearing on the wards and in the corridors of the hospital while she'd been there today, and it had been the same when she'd driven home along the quiet lanes where high in the trees there had been the rare sight of mistletoe, and down below every so often a bright red flash of holly, but there had been no joy in it. Christmas was just going to be something to be endured this year.

She'd thought of volunteering to work along with others over the Christmas weekend so that staff on the neuro unit with children could be with them, but the thought came that Ryan was one of them, and if he was caught up in any emergencies that couldn't be avoided, it would be catastrophic unless Mollie could be there for the children.

Saturday morning brought with it wintry sunshine, a chill wind, and the opportunity for her to carry on organising her new home as best she could with whatever was available in the form of resources.

She'd seen Ryan and the children go out on foot in the direction of the town centre, which was only a short walk away, while she had been putting curtains up at the dining-room window. She wished there was someone as close to her as his children were to him in spite of Martha's yearning for a mother.

Her own mother was long gone, her father had followed her just a short time ago, and she'd been an only child. As for her friends and the man she'd thought she was going to marry, none of them knew where she was and that was how she intended it to stay.

Having seen Ryan and the children strolling along happily had made her feel restless, and the chores that she'd had lined up were something that could be left for another day, so after showering and dressing carefully she ventured forth into the town centre.

It was a beautiful town, with its pump room and the well that produced the spa water from underground close by. There were hotels built out of weathered limestone that had a stately magnificence, gardens that stretched as far as the eye could see, and all around the small market town were the high peaks and green dales.

She came across Ryan and the girls on the pavement outside one of the toy shops and before she had a chance to backtrack Rhianna saw her so she had to stop.

'Hello, there,' he said easily, as if they were on the best of terms. 'Are you out Christmas shopping, too?' He then whispered, 'I've brought the children to have a look around the toy shop to get some ideas from what they show interest in, and then we're going to look for a wedding present for Mollie.'

'No,' she said in reply to his question. 'I haven't given Christmas a thought, or at least if I have they've been negative ones.'

He would have liked to ask her what she meant by that, but refrained with the children close by, and guessed that it would be something to do with her solitariness, which he supposed he could do something about if he was so inclined.

The children would love it if he asked Melissa to spend Christmas Day with them but what about him? Would having her there make the occasion a bigger ordeal or a lesser one?

Bringing his thoughts back to the present, he asked,

'Could you possibly stay here with the children for a moment while I go into the shop to check on how long delivery might be on some of the items they have on display?'

'Yes, of course,' she said, determined that there would be no repetition of the last time she'd been with them.

'We liked your sitting room, didn't we, Martha? But we think the rest of your house is ugly.' Rhianna piped up.

'Yes,' her sister agreed.

Melissa hid a smile. She was with them on that. It *was* ugly, but not for long, if not in time for Christmas maybe soon after.

'It was Daddy who told Mr Smethurst to put the carpet down on the floor for you,' Rhianna continued, and Melissa frowned. What was that supposed to mean?

'He told him not to tell you.'

'And why do you think that was?' Melissa asked gently.

'He said he would give him some money.'

So that was why the decorator hadn't wanted any extra payment for laying the carpet. Light was dawning.

Ryan stepped out of the shop at that moment, and leaving the children engrossed in what was in the window Melissa stepped quickly towards him and took him to one side.

'You paid for the carpet to be fitted, didn't you?' she choked out. 'I wondered why I wasn't charged any extra for it. It was very kind of you, Ryan, but please don't treat me as a charity case.'

'That is not how I see you,' he said levelly. 'I meant no offence. It was just a thought that it would give you pleasure to see the room finished when you came home, that's all.'

With that Ryan went to where the children were still observing the toy display and said, 'Say goodbye to Melissa.' And not allowing time for kisses and hugs this time, he walked them away from her and disappeared from sight.

There was a coffee shop nearby and Melissa went inside on leaden feet. As she stirred the drink in front of her unseeingly she was ashamed of her reaction to his kindness in one way but hurt that Ryan hadn't thought that he might have embarrassed her with his act of generosity.

He was the most attractive, amazing man she'd ever met, as well *as a paediatric surgeon* who was bringing up two motherless children with a totally selfless kind of love, and she'd dared to berate him for what to him had been just an act of thoughtfulness.

The urge for sightseeing was gone. She drank up quickly and made her way back to the crescent of town houses where they lived, feeling so ashamed of her behaviour she wouldn't be able to rest until she'd apologised. Ryan had shown her nothing but kindness since the day she'd arrived in Heatherdale and that was how she'd repaid him?

She would pop a note through his door so it was

there when he and the children arrived home from their Christmas shopping. For her part she intended to be nowhere to be seen. It would be time enough to face him when they met up on Monday morning at the hospital.

With every passing day she was becoming more aware of him and didn't want it to be like that because she knew that to him she was just someone he was allowing briefly into his busy life.

Ryan groaned when he read the note that was on his doormat when they got home. Their relationship, if it could be called that, was like a see-saw, up and down, but more down than up, and if he had any sense he ought to let it stay that way.

He had never met anyone to make him change his mind about marrying again, and if he ever did he hoped that it would be someone he knew something about. The children were his first consideration in everything he did because they were small and vulnerable, and if he was doing them no favours by not providing them with a new mother figure, at least he wasn't blotting out what little they remembered of Beth.

Tomorrow he would clear the air with Melissa, tell her that in future he would never again interfere in her affairs, and if the promise made life less liveable he would have to stick with it.

She wasn't around on the Sunday, as he'd been expecting, and he felt frustrated and on edge, eager to say his piece and clarify the situation between them knowing that he wasn't going to rest until he'd said it.

But short of talking into thin air he was going to have to wait until she reappeared.

He wasn't to know that she was at the last place he would have expected. She'd seen a notice in the hospital announcing that there was to be a children's Christmas party for past and present young patients on Sunday and that volunteers to assist from staff and friends were needed.

On impulse she'd given her name to the organisers during the week and after Saturday's upset was grateful to have somewhere to go where she could be lost in a crowd, instead of being isolated in her grandmother's house.

She'd checked to make sure that Ryan wouldn't be there and been told that consultants didn't usually take part on such occasions, that it was organised by the nurses and social workers based at the hospital. It would start mid-morning and finish halfway through the afternoon.

The party was a yearly event that was held in the run-up to Christmas, and when she arrived Melissa felt as if she belonged for the first time since she'd come to Heatherdale.

For the children who were confined to bed there was special attention to their needs and she was perched on the side of the bed of a small girl who'd had surgery a few days previously after a fall that had resulted in bleeding inside her head.

They were playing one of the fun games that had been provided and the little one was forgetting her tears and fears in the excitement of the party when Melissa looked up and her eyes widened. Ryan and his children had just arrived and he was chatting to one of the nurses.

He hadn't seen her, but Rhianna and Martha had. They'd left their father's side and were coming across the ward to her.

Ryan looked up at that moment and surprise showed on his face.

This was the last place he would have expected to find Melissa. Weekdays yes, but not on a Sunday. He wouldn't be here himself if it hadn't been that just an hour ago he'd had some bad news that could affect the neurology unit during coming days. He'd driven to the hospital to check on what his clinics and surgery arrangements were for the coming week.

A phone call had come through from Julian's parents to inform him that their son had been involved in a riding accident the previous day and was in a Manchester hospital with spinal injuries.

'It looks as if it might be a long job,' Julian's father had told Ryan and he'd thought that Melissa had arrived in the unit in the nick of time. She was going to be heaven sent in his working life—*and could be the same out of it if he would only let her.*

There was no use denying it. Melissa was never out of his mind no matter how much he told himself that she was just a passing fancy. His children loved her and who could blame them? There was a gentleness about her when she was with them that pulled at his heartstrings, but did she feel the same about him? He doubted it. She seemed to have enough emotional dramas of her own to worry about, without taking on those of a bereaved father!

The phone call had brought him to the hospital to check what was on their agenda in the unit for the coming week with Julian missing, and here *she* was, conveniently already on hospital premises.

'Will you excuse me for a moment?' he asked the nurse beside him. 'I see my colleague over there, chatting to my daughters, and I need to speak to her. Dr Tindall has had a serious riding accident and we need to check what we have ahead of us in the coming week.

'Can you look after Elfrida for a few moments while I talk to Melissa?' he asked Rhianna and Martha, indicating the small girl in the bed, and when they nodded he told her in a low voice, 'Julian isn't going to be around for some time. He's been seriously injured in a riding accident so it is going to be all systems go here next week and for some time to come.

'I'm here because I need to know what I'm down for in the clinics and theatre and I can get that information from my secretary's computer, so I'm going to have a quick look. Finding you here has saved me having to disturb you at home so can I leave the children with you for a little while?'

'Yes, of course,' she told him. She had listened to what he'd had to say in stunned silence, aghast to hear what had happened to Julian, with her first thought for the hospital's Romeo. Then it dawned on her that it was going to be just the two of them working together for the foreseeable future until a temporary replacement could be found.

They were going to be in each other's company workwise much more than she'd expected. How was she going to cope with that? How was she going to keep a hold on the attraction he had for her, being near him so much in the neuro unit and only a few yards away from him at home?

But most importantly, would Ryan want her around him so much? He might feel that living next door to her was enough, especially after her having been so ungrateful about the carpet-laying incident.

After flicking through his appointment list on the computer, he returned to Melissa and the girls.

'So what do you think about Julian? What a shame, eh?' he commented.

'Yes, it is,' she said in a low voice. 'I have had no wish to go back to Manchester since I moved here, but will put all that to one side and go to visit him when I get the chance.'

'Me too,' he agreed. 'I'm going to have plenty to keep me occupied for some time to come, but will find time for that.' He looked around him. 'How long are you planning on staying at the party?'

'I'm not sure,' she told him. 'It depends on how long I'm needed.'

'Right, we'll be off, then,' he said, and with a child on either side of him he went.

Melissa could tell that Rhianna and Martha were disappointed that she wasn't leaving at the same time as them, but she knew the rules now and number one was '*no fussing please*', so she waved them off with a bright smile that faded as soon as they'd disappeared.

Outside in the hospital corridor Ryan hesitated. He was going to take the children for a meal somewhere and was tempted to ask Melissa to join them. He wanted to make amends for their exchange of words outside the toy shop. Turning, he took the children back into the ward and saw that the party was practically over. Relatives of the children were helping nursing staff to tidy the place and Melissa was ready for the off, expecting that he would have gone by now.

'What's wrong, Ryan? I thought you'd gone.'

'We're going for a meal in the children's favourite restaurant,' he explained, 'and I wondered if you would like to join us.' It was a spur-of-the-moment invitation and he expected her to refuse.

'Yes, I would like to very much,' she told him, 'just as long as you are sure you want me there.'

'I wouldn't have asked you otherwise,' he said easily. 'I'll lead the way in my car, with you following, if that's all right?'

'Yes,' she replied.

She noticed that his expression didn't alter when

Rhianna cried, 'Goody! Melissa is coming with us, Martha!'

When they were seated at a table in a bright modern restaurant with the children tucking in to fish fingers and chips and the adults something more spectacular, Ryan amazed her by commenting in a low voice, 'This is what I miss, family outings. We used to do this a lot when Beth was with us, but it all feels like a charade now.'

'Maybe it does,' Melissa said carefully, 'but you are the only one who can put that right, Ryan. You are a fantastic father, holding down a very responsible job, but you must feel the loss of your wife a great deal. What was she like? Tell me about her.'

'Beth was just Beth, medium height, slim and very active, with brown eyes like the children's and light brown hair. She was a loving mother and dedicated to bringing babies safely into the world. Wouldn't hear of it when I tried to persuade her not to go out in the storm, and that was how she lost her life.'

When he lapsed into silence Melissa asked gently, 'And would she not want you to have the joys of family life again with someone else?'

'Maybe' was the answer. 'But so far there has been no one that I've wanted enough to be ready to take that step.' Until now, maybe? But he was far from sure that it would be a good idea to give Melissa any signals that he might regret afterwards.

Even though today had shown an affinity between them that hadn't been there before. Maybe it was because this was his loneliest time of the year, and whatever her Christmastimes had been like in the past, this one looked as if it was going to be a non-event.

The waitress was at his elbow, waiting to take orders for dessert, and the conversation became general again until they were leaving the place and Rhianna spotted mistletoe above the doorway.

'Look, Daddy!' she cried, and lifted her face to be kissed beneath the white berries. When he'd bent to oblige it was Martha's turn, and as he straightened up she cried, 'Melissa hasn't had a kiss! She must have one too!'

As Melissa shook her head laughingly, Ryan stepped towards her and took her in his arms. He wished the moment could go on for ever because the feel of her mouth under his and the closeness of her was like coming in out of the cold.

When he let her go there was a round of applause from the other diners and taking her hand, with Rhianna on one side and Martha on the other, they left the restaurant with not a word between them and went to their separate cars.

On arriving home, Ryan unlocked the door to let the children in. Before going inside himself, he walked over to where Melissa stood at her own front door.

'Do I have to say sorry for what happened?'

'No,' she said lightly, 'not at all. It was only a Christmas kiss, wasn't it?'

'Yes, of course,' he replied with a tight smile, and was gone. After his door had closed behind him, Melissa went inside and sank down onto the nearest chair. She relived the moments in his arms again. Beyond that she couldn't think.

CHAPTER FIVE

IT HAD BEEN the strangest of weekends as far as Melissa was concerned. She wasn't sure what to think as she drove to the hospital on the Monday morning. First there'd been her exchange of words with Ryan outside the toy shop about the carpet-laying, and the consequent remorse on her part for being so ungracious when she'd tackled him about it.

Then, thinking she had been well away from him when she'd gone to help with the party, he had turned up there with the bad news about Julian and had left her uneasy about what it could mean for them both. Finally there had been that surprise dinner invitation, culminating in an unexpectedly passionate kiss!

Monday morning was always Ryan's first clinic of the week and even though Melissa was early he was there before her and observed her keenly for a second when she appeared.

'If you do the ward rounds, I'll get going with the clinic earlier than usual,' he said briskly. So much for their kiss under the mistletoe. He was finished before her and came to join her as she moved from bed to bed, where often anxious parents were hovering, seeking reassurance.

Ryan was impressed with what he saw. Melissa was a natural with patients and parents. Obviously he'd seen her in this mode before and was satisfied with the way she performed, but today his awareness of her was heightened. He'd spent the night tossing and turning, the memory of their kiss haunting him. It should have been a peck on the cheek and it hadn't been. It had opened a floodgate of longing that he wanted to hold back, but the more he observed her the harder it became.

Unaware of how his mind was working, Melissa was concentrating on the young occupants of the beds in the two wards. She was confident that it was here that she belonged, amongst children who were sick and needed all the help they could get to become well again.

As the young ones and the parents hovering around their beds saw her approaching they felt her reaching out to them. No matter how worrying the diagnosis they had been given previously or might be receiving, she made them feel that their child was special.

'So,' Ryan said when the rounds were over. 'Now we'll leave the wards in the care of the nursing staff and have a quick lunch. This afternoon you can watch and learn while I operate on a child with a cleft lip and palate, just as long as there aren't any emergencies brought into A and E that our unit have to deal with.'

She was expecting Ryan to lunch in his office as he'd done on other days since she'd joined the staff of the neuro unit, but when she moved in the direction of the staff restaurant he fell into step beside her and when they'd queued and been served he said, 'Do you mind if I join you?'

'No, of course not,' she told him. She hoped he wasn't going to refer to the mistletoe incident while they were eating. It would be just too embarrassing if he did as she hadn't been entirely unresponsive while he'd been kissing her.

She needn't have concerned herself. He made no mention of it. He was probably regretting it and had decided to act as if it had never happened.

When they'd finished eating, Ryan got to his feet and said, 'I usually have a quick chat with Mollie in the lunch hour to check that the children got off to school all right, so will you excuse me? They were chattering non-stop about yesterday at breakfast-time.'

Before she could ask what part of the day before he was referring to, he was wending his way towards the restaurant exit.

He was an exceptional man. Strong and caring when it came to those he loved, and professionally a doctor of complete dedication to his calling. When she compared him to the man she'd been going to marry she felt grateful now instead of bitter that David had called off their engagement. It was all because of the man who'd taken her under his wing when she'd come crawling to Heatherdale like a lost soul.

She still had no idea what Ryan really thought about her, of course. However delightful he was to work with, nothing had changed back at the town houses where they lived. When he came home from the hospital each night she didn't see him until the following morning and so she had to be satisfied with that. However, she did wish she had the chance to see the children more often, even if their father was still guarding his private life just as much as before.

On the Saturday of her second week on the neuro unit, Melissa planned to visit Julian at the hospital where he was recovering. It was against the vow she'd made never to return to Manchester, but she felt so sorry that Julian's career and future had been put at risk by such a dreadful accident that the least she could do was take him some magazines, nice things to eat, and give him a few hours of her time.

She was undecided whether to tell Ryan what she was intending, or just proceed with her arrangements. In the end decided to just go and tell him afterwards.

'Wow!' Julian said when he saw Melissa approaching his bedside and to his parents who were present.

'This is a surprise! Mum, Dad, may I introduce Melissa? She's a doctor on my neuro unit.'

They smiled across at her.

'So, how are you coping without my charm and expertise?' he teased.

She had to smile at the question. Only Julian would be so chirpy while flat on his back with a spinal injury.

'Everyone is hoping that it won't be long before you are back amongst us.'

She could hear footsteps on the polished floor behind her and children's voices, and when Julian exclaimed, 'Look who's here now!' she turned slowly and saw Ryan coming towards them with Rhianna and Martha in tow.

When the children saw her they ran to her side, and Martha asked, 'How did you know we were coming?'

'I didn't,' she told her gently, 'but it's a lovely surprise.'

'We knocked on your door to ask you if you wanted to come with us,' Rhianna explained, 'but you weren't there. Why are you never there when we want you, Melissa?'

Ryan was chatting to Julian after greeting his parents and wasn't a part of her conversation with the children, but Melissa knew he'd heard what Rhianna had said, although he was still smiling at the chirpy patient on the bed.

'I'm hungry, Melissa,' Martha said pleadingly, taking Melissa's hand.

'I'll take them to the snack bar near the main entrance for something to eat while you talk to Julian,' she told Ryan. 'And I promise not to lose them,' she teased gently. Before he had time to reply they were off with smiles from her two young companions and a level look in her direction from their father.

* * *

As Ryan watched Melissa and the girls walk away, he was filled with mixed emotions. On the one hand, it was heart-warming to see how easily and openly his girls responded to her. On the other, it made him feel things he wasn't yet ready to feel. Was he attracted to her? He thought he probably was, but was he ready to do anything about that attraction? And what about letting the girls get too close? He was on dangerous ground.

'So where are you off to when you leave here?' Julian asked, breaking into his thoughts. His parents had gone to do some shopping while he had someone to talk to and Ryan brought his thoughts back to the present as Julian continued to chat.

'They tell me that the Christmas lights are on everywhere in the city centre and that there are Father Christmases appearing in all the big stores. Your children will want to visit him, won't they?'

'Yes, I'm sure they will,' he agreed. 'I hope that you will soon be mobile again, Julian. If our hospital wasn't just for children, we could have had you recovering in Heatherdale.'

'I'll do my best,' he promised. 'Besides, you'll be all right with Melissa filling my slot. How lucky can you get?'

Ryan's smile was twisted. 'I don't know. It's debatable.'

Melissa's appearance in his life had brought chaos rather than tranquillity into the ordered existence that was the only way he could survive his many responsibilities of family and work. But at night, in the darkness, in his lonely bedroom, when all the house was still, visions of her came to mind.

The long dark mane of her hair, the mouth that was never anything but tender when she was with his children, but buttoned up if *he* ever tried to get to know her better, and the dark hazel eyes that were full of hurt and loneliness.

She was in his line of vision at the top of the ward, bringing the children back from the snack bar, and as he was going to take Rhianna and Martha to see Santa Claus in one of the big stores it seemed only fitting that he should invite her to go with them rather than let Melissa make the train journey home on her own.

'Do you want to come with us to tell Santa Claus what you want for Christmas?' he asked her as the three of them drew level.

Julian had just been taken for a scan and as Melissa surveyed the empty bed she had a question of her own. 'Where's Julian?' she asked anxiously.

'Gone for a scan. He said to pass on his goodbyes,' he replied laconically. So much for his invitation. Could it possibly be that Melissa was attracted in another direction?

Melissa smiled, the moment of anxiety past. 'Yes, I'd love to see Santa.' There were a few things she would like for her first Christmas in Heatherdale, top of the list a better understanding with her independent neighbour.

As they left the hospital, Ryan's thoughts were running on a different track. He was remembering that Mollie wouldn't be around to cook the Christmas dinner for them as she usually did. She and Jack were getting married on the morning of Christmas Eve and they were off to Italy later in the day for their honeymoon. He was going to have to polish up his cooking skills.

He was still doubtful about asking Melissa to share the most festive day of the year with them as he knew she would pick up on his sadness and see his tension. Yet for all he knew she might have plans of her own on how to spend the day. Although she hadn't exactly been bubbling with joy when Christmas had first been mentioned. But spending it in a house that had only one presentable room was not a tempting prospect.

They found a jovial Santa in the first of the big stores that they came to amongst the busy city throng. Excitedly, Rhianna couldn't wait to tell him exactly what she wanted this Christmas.

'There are lots of things we would like,' she told him, 'but most of all we want a mummy.'

Santa's white brows lifted. It was obvious he wasn't too sure how to react to that one!

'Why don't you make a list and send it to me?' he said. 'One of my fairies will give you my address.'

Rhianna seemed satisfied with that and the small party made their way from the store.

'I'm sorry that you had to be involved in yet another

awkward moment,' Ryan said. His tone was casual, as if it had been something and nothing.

Melissa was unaware that, inside, Ryan was cringing at another plea from his children for someone to take Beth's place. She smiled.

'Think nothing of it,' she told him. 'What the children are asking for is quite understandable, but anyone can see how well cared for and happy they are. You are a man in a million.'

'Most folks think I'm a fool,' he replied dryly. 'Struggling on alone.'

She was the fool for imagining that one day he might turn to her.

They worked together, doing what they'd been trained for, and it was a joy. They lived next door to each other, and if they weren't always communicating under those circumstances she was always conscious of his nearness.

Any imaginings of what it might be like to have him beside her in the night were kept under control. Ryan was a man who was travelling along a road of his own making and didn't want company on the way. What about herself? Hadn't she vowed to steer clear of the opposite sex too?

Unaware of Melissa's thoughts, Ryan was wishing that those few moments in the store when Rhianna had turned a happy occasion into a depressing one had never happened, but as they had the atmosphere between Melissa and himself needed lightening.

'Shall we go for a meal before we go for the train, somewhere bright and festive?'

'That would be lovely,' she replied. Her glance held his for a precious moment and he smiled.

'Let's go, then,' he said briskly, and with Martha holding Melissa's hand tightly amongst the crowds, and Rhianna clinging to her father, they went to find a place to eat.

'You know the city better than I do, so you choose,' he suggested as they moved along. 'How far are we from where you used to live?' He saw the brightness fade from her face.

'Not far enough,' she replied flatly, and pointed to a restaurant that had an attractive menu displayed. 'I think that your young ones will like this place.'

So much for Melissa telling him anything about herself that he didn't already know. Yet why should she tell him about her life before Heatherdale if she didn't want to? It didn't make him feel any less curious.

'Melissa!' a voice exclaimed from nearby. 'I've been wondering where you'd got to.' When Ryan looked up he saw an expensively dressed older woman looking down at them.

'And now you know,' Melissa replied coolly. 'How are you, Monica?'

'Er, I'm fine, busy getting ready for David's big day. It's going to be the wedding of the year in our set.' The other woman's glance went over Ryan and the girls. 'I see you haven't been moping.'

'Dr Ferguson is my boss, and these are his children.'

'Ah. I see,' Monica said with a meaningful smile that belied the words.

'I don't think you do,' Melissa told her. Her face was drained of colour but she remained totally calm.

Ryan was curious about the identity of this woman who was interrupting their meal. She was going, thank goodness!

'It has been nice to meet you, Dr...er... And what lovely children.'

Uninterested, Rhianna and Martha tucked into the food that had just arrived, but as the other woman floated off, Melissa's calm deserted her and she bent her head as a flood of painful memories came back of the weeks and months before she'd moved to Heatherdale.

As he watched her Ryan felt like following that Monica woman and throttling her. He didn't know who she was to Melissa, but it was clear that she was bad news as far as she was concerned.

'I wouldn't mind knowing who that was,' he said gently, and this time Melissa didn't hesitate to reply.

'She was going to be my mother-in-law until her son broke off our engagement.'

'Of course, I remember you telling me that you were escaping a broken engagement. I hope you don't think that all men are that shallow, Melissa? He obviously didn't deserve you.'

'No, of course I don't think that.' she said quickly. 'It's very kind of you to take my side so readily.'

If she didn't feel that the new rapport that the day

had brought between them might be spoilt, she would have told him that if she *had* felt like that, getting to know him would have made her think again. She couldn't help but admire the choices he'd made when he'd lost his wife, and she was deeply moved by his gentleness with sick children. She felt privileged to know him.

They finished their meal quickly, the girls' excited chatter filling any potentially uncomfortable silences between Melissa and Ryan.

On the train journey home the two of them were again silent, but the children continued to make up for it. Used to being in the car, the novelty of a journey by train or bus caused great excitement and Melissa had to smile.

She'd been brought up with expensive cars and still used that form of transport, but now it was a small second-hand car. Where at first it had been a wrench to see them go, now it didn't seem to matter as long as she arrived at her destination.

She would have liked to invite the three of them in for some supper when they arrived back in Heatherdale, basic as her accommodation was, but she knew if Ryan came up with a reason not to accept the invitation it would take the edge off the brief closeness.

As they parked their respective cars and approached their own doors, Ryan was reluctant for the day to end.

'Would you like to come in for a coffee?'

'Are you sure?' she asked in surprise. 'I'd considered

asking you the same thing but didn't want to cause embarrassment if you refused for some reason.'

He *wasn't* sure, far from it! As she'd walked along level with him he'd watched the dark swathe of her hair swing gently against her shoulders and had wanted to hold her close, tell her that she had no need to be so alone any more.

If she needed someone he would be there, next door, ready to help. Yet would he be able to fulfil that promise on a purely friendly basis and not begin to want more? If he had any sense he would let Melissa get on with her own life now that she was settled here and was no longer unemployed. He should take a back seat and take pleasure from working with her.

She was excellent at her job, quick to learn, efficient in every aspect of paediatrics, and their young patients responded well to her, without alarm, but he hadn't answered her question.

He could tell her glibly that, yes, he was sure, because he didn't want the day to end just yet. Their relationship had moved on, he'd felt it in every word she'd said, in her every movement, but he wasn't sure that he was ready to let Beth be just a beautiful memory, instead of keeping to the vows he'd made on the day she'd been lowered gently into a grave in the churchyard.

Melissa watched him, wondering when his thoughts were going to come back from where they'd gone. He'd opened the front door to let the children into the house and for what seemed like an eternity she'd been waiting for him to say something as she had a strong feeling that he was regretting his impulsive invitation.

Sure enough, he turned to face her.

'Maybe we *should* call it a day, Melissa. The children are usually tucked up in bed by this time. But I want you to know that if ever you have a problem I'll always be only too pleased to help if needed.'

'I can cope, Ryan,' she told him levelly. 'The past few months have taught me a lot about myself and I feel stronger than ever. I'm hoping that most of my problems will be over once I've got the house how I want it. So please don't feel that you need to increase your commitments by adding me to the list.'

On that comment she opened her own door and went inside, and as he watched it close behind her Ryan's heart sank. What was he playing at? He'd invited her to have coffee and then gone back on it, and had been extremely patronising with his offer of help.

He was the one in need, content on the outside unhappy on the inside. Mollie had ventured to tell him a few times that Beth would not want him to live like this and he'd just ignored her advice and let it pass.

But on those occasions he hadn't known that there was such a person as Melissa Redmond and now he did. Not only was she one of the best registrars he'd ever worked with, she was his neighbour. Were the fates telling him something? Not if they knew that once he made up his mind regarding something important he rarely changed it!

CHAPTER SIX

IT WAS SUNDAY again. This was the day that Melissa always felt was long and empty. Well, not empty—she had plenty of chores she could get to. Still, her life did feel empty of family and friends because there was no one to phone her, or come to her door, except Ryan, of course, and after her cool reception of his change of mind the night before she wasn't expecting that. Part of her was almost dreading seeing him at work in the morning, too.

What had he expected her to do once the children had fallen asleep and they had been alone? Strip off and do the dance of the seven veils? One thing was sure, he would be keeping a low profile today after her chilly acceptance of his speedy change of mind.

She was wrong. He phoned at midday.

'Have you ever done any knitting, Melissa?'

'Not since I was about twelve,' she informed him. 'Why do you ask? Are you short of something to do in your spare time?'

'Hardly! Explain to me, what is spare time?'

'I've heard it described as the time you wish you had but never get. So tell me more about the knitting.'

'Rhianna wants to knit her doll a wetsuit. But first she has to learn how to knit.'

'Has she got a pattern, wool, and needles?'

'Er…no.'

'Right, so if you will entrust her to me, the two of us will go to the shops today and sort that out, if any of those kinds of places are open on a Sunday.'

'No problem regarding that,' he told her. 'Heatherdale is a popular tourist centre. They come from miles around to see the spa, the well and the rest. Sunday is one of the busiest days for the shops, but are you sure you can spare the time to take Rhianna for the wool and stuff?'

Could she spare the time? Of course she could. Ryan was actually willing to let Rhianna out of his sight for a while *and into her keeping*!

'Yes,' she told him, 'but a wetsuit is rather ambitious for a first attempt. Beginners usually start with something simple, like maybe a scarf for their doll?'

He was laughing. 'We Fergusons always aim high— in endeavour that is.'

She didn't join in. Was he referring to his dedication to his job or his celibate life or both?

'So shall I send Rhianna round?'

'Yes, but, Ryan, what about Martha? Won't she want to come?'

'No, she's all right, watching a children's film on TV at the moment.

'Thanks for offering to take Rhianna for whatever she needs to get started, and being willing to spend some time with her.'

'Thanks are not necessary,' she told him. 'It will be a pleasure, *not a chore*,' she continued coolly.

'Yes, of course,' Ryan said hastily. He'd phoned her with the request about the knitting because he'd been desperate to hear her voice after his bungled invitation. He was getting the kind of reception he deserved, though, looking on the bright side, Melissa hadn't hesitated when she'd heard what he'd rung for. He said a brief goodbye and went to tell Rhianna the good news.

As he watched the two of them walking along the pavement in the direction of the town centre, Ryan swallowed hard. They looked so right together, with Rhianna chattering away to Melissa and doing a little skip every few steps, but not as right as if it had been Beth taking her daughter to the shops. Would that feeling of loss ever go away?

They weren't gone long and then they were back. Melissa phoned to say that she was giving Rhianna her first knitting lesson and would send her back shortly. She'd also managed to talk Rhianna out of the wetsuit and into the idea of knitting her doll a scarf for starters.

'Sounds great,' he said. He wished Melissa was there beside him so that he could have the pleasure of her company, instead of having only her voice to listen to, but thankfully there was still tomorrow to look forward to at the hospital, where they had no hang-ups around each other.

* * *

Melissa saw Mollie arrive earlier than usual while she was having her breakfast the next morning, and within minutes Ryan was on the phone.

'Emergency Services are bringing in two youngsters with serious head injuries from a pile-up on the motorway. Eleven-year-old twin boys who were in the back seat of the family car without seat belts. They were thrown forward like rag dolls when the car behind them in the pile-up connected with the back of theirs. It's the tail end of the night shift so they're hanging on for the moment. Needless to say, I want to be there when they bring them in, so I'm off now. Can you follow as soon as possible? If surgery is required, I'll want you to assist.'

'Yes, of course,' she told him, already stepping out of her nightdress on her way to the bathroom. The adrenaline was kicking in. This was what she'd trained for, and it was going to be under the guidance of Ryan Ferguson. Did anything else matter?

If he was going to throw a fit every time she was near enough for the other kind of physical contact that had nothing to do with medicine and everything to do with sexual chemistry, at least she would have these kinds of moments to treasure.

Ryan was in Theatre, scrubbed up and masked, when she got there. He pointed to a motionless young figure on the operating table.

'Both twins have frontal fractures of the skull due to the force with which they were thrown forward, but this young guy is the most serious so I'm going to operate on him first. The other lad is next door, being watched over by theatre staff. The anaesthetist is at the ready so get gowned up and then we'll begin.

'The two boys had arrived and been scanned by the time I got here. It has shown there's a subdural haemorrhage to deal with for this youngster. He has been barely conscious since it happened, so I don't want to delay as there's bleeding between the inner surface of the skull and the outer layer of the meninges. Have you been involved with anything like this before?'

'Only once, but I remember it clearly,' Melissa told him. 'Just tell me what to do and I'll do it.'

As she scrubbed up, in what could not have been a more unexpected moment, Melissa realised that she was falling for Ryan, the golden-haired consultant who had burst into her life like a breath of clean fresh air. She loved his integrity, his devotion to his children, and to those belonging to others who came into his care, and above all his loyalty to his dead wife.

Would he ever feel the same way about her? There was a spark between them that would soon become a flame given the chance.

Ryan was waiting. The theatre nurses were in position, the anaesthetist poised for action at the head of the operating table and everything became centred on saving the life of an injured child.

Later in the morning the process was repeated for the second boy with the same sort of injury as his brother.

It seemed that they'd been on their way to school, with their mother driving, and with the carelessness of youth had skipped fastening their seat belts, which had caused not only devastation for themselves but a nightmare for her too.

Just before three o'clock in the afternoon the theatre staff were having a welcome late lunch in the staff restaurant after the traumas of the morning. It wasn't unusual, they often had to eat when they got the chance. Ryan had chosen to have a bite in his office as he wanted to make his regular call home to check that Mollie had coped all right with the Monday morning rush for the children.

The two boys had been transferred to the high-dependency unit, where they were being monitored all the time by nursing staff and watched over by their horrified parents, whose normal Monday morning had turned into a nightmare.

When Ryan had spoken to Mollie he went to seek out Melissa, who was in the middle of a late ward round. He found her sitting by the side of the cot of a tearful two-year-old whose mother had just taken an older child to the toilet. She was holding his hand and soothing him gently. Melissa was fantastic, either on the job or off it. So why couldn't he act on that delightful thought and do something about it, instead of holding on to the past so tightly?

'When you've finished rounds, I'd like a quick word

in my office,' he said briskly to conceal the effect she was having on him.

She smiled up at him. 'Yes, of course, Dr Ferguson.' She pointed to the toddler who was now asleep, still holding her hand. 'I'll just let Oscar settle into a deeper sleep before I move away.'

'Of course.' When a nurse approached with the medicines trolley he went.

The nurse was middle-aged, plump with a smiley face, and as she observed his departing straight-backed and purposeful figure, she said with comic wistfulness, 'Isn't he something to make any woman's heart beat faster?

'I keep telling my husband that if he doesn't stop watching football on the television instead of taking me out, I'm going to run off with Dr Ferguson. Which might not be so easy as our doctor friend is reluctant to put any woman in place of that nice wife of his.'

The nurse went on her way, moving from bed to bed with whatever medication its young occupant might be requiring. Melissa was despondent. To be told what she had already worked out for herself had put a blight on the day.

When she went to Ryan's office the first thing she saw was a florist's delivery of beautiful flowers of the season on a side table. Picking up the bouquet, he got to his feet and came round to her side of his desk and handed them to her.

'Just to say thanks for putting Rhianna on the right track with the knitting. There wasn't a sound out of her last night. She was working away at it until the very last moment before going to bed and at breakfast before I left the house. So thanks, Melissa.'

She looked down at the flowers and swallowed hard. It was the moment to tell him that she would do lots more for his children and *him* if he would let her, that she was falling in love with him, he was in her every waking thought *and in her dreams*, but something held her back.

She was letting a nice gesture mean more than had been meant by it. Her dealings with her ex-fiancé had shown her that humiliation was a hard pill to swallow if she should be mistaken, and hadn't the medicines nurse just confirmed Ryan's devotion to his wife's memory?

'You didn't have to do this, Ryan. I enjoyed the time spent with your daughter, but thanks, anyway.'

As she turned to go he stopped her.

'There is one other thing.'

She swivelled round to face him once more.

'You were good in Theatre this morning. We work well together. Keep it up and you will have a great future before you in paediatrics.'

'Maybe,' she told him gravely, 'but somewhere along the way I want to be a wife and mother, too.'

She watched him flinch.

'Yes, of course,' he agreed stiffly, and went back to the paperwork on his desk, leaving her to make an undignified exit. Once out of his office she went through a side door that led to the car park and put the flowers in her car out of sight. There was no way she wanted questions asked about them by other staff that might set rumours off that were not true.

The twin boys from the motorway accident had re-gained consciousness when she returned to the neuro unit and were looking pale, drowsy, and rather the worse for wear. Unless anything unforeseen occurred, they should, however, make full recoveries.

During their separate operations they'd had burr holes drilled into their skulls and blood clots drained away, followed by repair of damaged blood vessels.

As she checked them over their father said som-brely, 'Somehow I don't think they'll forget to fasten their seat belts again.'

When Melissa went to her car at the end of the day Ryan was about to drive off in his and he rolled the window down.

'You know that Mollie is getting married to Jack on the morning of Christmas Eve and that Rhianna and Martha are to be her attendants? She was saying the other day that she wondered if you would be willing to help in the choosing of their dresses.'

'Me!' she exclaimed. 'But I hardly know your house-keeper.'

'She may not be that for much longer, I fear, cer-tainly not in the same capacity. Come the new year I might have to find a substitute, but that's a few weeks away yet. So, getting back to the wedding and the chil-dren, Mollie would be glad of your advice as you wear such attractive clothes yourself.'

She smiled. How ironic.

'My clothes belong to a time when I was a pampered pet and I haven't been able to afford anything new since, but while I've come to live in Heatherdale I've forgiven my father. In a strange sort of way he did me a favour when I had to sell the place we had in Cheshire and come to live in my grandmother's house.' *Because if it hadn't happened I would never have met you,* she wanted to tell him, but she was still too cautious. The dread of being hurt again was like a dark shadow hanging over her

'It's good to know that you're happy here!' he exclaimed. 'I've had my doubts about that once or twice. I have always felt that this is a magical place, but I don't expect everyone to feel the same as I do.'

With an unmistakeable lift to his voice he continued, 'Getting back to the matter of Mollie's wedding, can I tell her that you'll go with her to choose the children's dresses? She is concerned that they should have something really pretty but also warm and cosy for this time of year. I can usually manage to choose their clothes myself, while giving them some degree of choice, but not when it is something like this, and in winter.'

'Yes, of course. I'll help in any way I can,' she said. Was she in her right mind, surrounding herself with the trappings of motherhood when their father ran a mile if she came within touching distance?

'Thanks, Melissa, that's wonderful. I am most grateful,' he told her, still smiling, and added jokingly, 'I've got my name down for a knitted pullover when Rhianna is more accomplished in the art.'

She smiled back at him. 'Don't tease her, Ryan. She is more like you than you realise, not to be defeated by anything, but she is only seven years old.'

He didn't reply, just gave her a long level look, and she wondered if he thought her interfering. He brought the subject back to Mollie's wedding.

'The way things are going, we Fergusons are going to be well represented on the day as not only are the girls going to be Mollie's young attendants, she has asked me to give her away as she has no close family. Her husband died a few years ago and she has no sons or daughters to do the honours, so it will be my pleasure.

'Her invitation was addressed to Ryan Ferguson, family, and friend, so if you want to tag along with us, Melissa, feel free. You will be most welcome.'

'Thanks just the same but no,' she said levelly, not enamoured by the phrasing of his invitation. 'I am not a tag-along sort of person. My life has scraped the bottom of the barrel over recent months and one of the things it has taught me is not to accept being merely tolerated by anyone.'

She watched his eyes widen and his jaw tighten. She drove off before he had a chance to comment. If he had, Ryan would have told her that he'd phrased the invitation in such a manner because he didn't know what Melissa thought of him, and a casual approach had seemed like the best idea at this stage of their relationship.

What would she have said if he'd worded it along the lines that she was the best thing that had happened to him in years and he would be proud to have her by his side in front of Mollie and her wedding guests?

The rest of the week dragged by on leaden feet.

On the day that Ryan was holding one of his clinics Melissa asked, 'Is there a chance that I could sit in with you as I did when I first came onto the ward? I learned such a lot.'

'I'm glad to hear it,' he said with a dry smile, 'but I think not at present. If Julian was here there would be no problem, but as it is I need you on the wards while I'm taking the clinic so that all aspects of the job are covered. I don't know if he will ever be mobile enough to come back to us but if he eventually does...'

'What?' she asked. '*What* if he eventually does? Are you going to tell me I might be out of a job? Do you want me gone?'

'Now you are being ridiculous,' he told her, and almost laughed.

As if!

She was the best registrar he'd ever had. How could Melissa ever think that he would pass her over because of a few wrongly chosen words in the car park the other night? He just had the feeling that he needed to cool it for a while. After all, their small patients came first.

* * *

It was Saturday. The small town was buzzing with Christmas shoppers and a local brass band played carols in the centre of the town square beside the huge Christmas tree.

As she heard the music in the distance, Melissa remembered Ryan telling her about the musical event some time previously. When she saw the three of them come out of the house next door and move off in that direction, she decided to go to the special yearly happening herself, but from another direction to avoid being invited to *tag along.*

It wasn't likely, of course, not after the reception the wording of his invitation had received that evening in the hospital car park, but she wasn't taking any chances. She was relieved that Ryan wasn't going to be present later in the afternoon when the promised shopping trip with Mollie and his children was to take place.

There were lots of the townsfolk gathered around the tree and as the band played the familiar music and those there sang the equally familiar words, she looked around her at the beautiful setting and sent up a prayer of thanks to the fates that had brought her here.

It was as if Manchester, the place that had been so familiar to her with its smart stores and many famous restaurants, didn't exist, and neither did the millionaire's row where she had lived with her father on money owed to others.

For the first time in ages she was beginning to feel

in control of her life. That the house was still dark and dismal except for her delightful sitting room didn't matter—she would get that sorted eventually. She had the job she'd always longed for in pleasant surroundings and had met a man who made all others seem nondescript.

The only cloud in her sky was that she doubted he saw her in the same light, though why should he when he was still in love with the wife who had been taken from him so tragically?

A child's voice calling her name broke into her thoughts and when she looked up there was Ryan with his girls, all three smiling their surprise at seeing her amongst the festive crowd.

'Hello, there,' Ryan said. 'I nearly phoned to remind you of the band playing carols before we left the house as I wasn't sure if you remembered me mentioning it a couple of weeks ago.'

Unable to disguise her pleasure at meeting them, she told him, 'I'd forgotten but when the sound of the music came drifting over I realised where it was coming from and came to see what was going on.'

She turned to Rhianna and Martha.

'Are you ready for us going shopping this afternoon for your dresses for Mollie's wedding?'

'Yes,' they chorused excitedly.

Martha added, 'We already know what kind we want, Melissa.'

'Really!' she said in mock surprise.

'So be prepared,' Ryan warned laughingly, and followed it by saying, 'We are about to go for a hot drink somewhere. Dare I ask if you'd like to join us?'

There was no mention of her 'tagging along', she noticed as their glances met, but she knew he wouldn't have forgotten and she wished she hadn't been so snappy the other night in the car park.

'I'd love to,' she told him, letting the joy of being with the three of them take over. It diminished somewhat as they strolled along the high street in the direction of a café in one of the parks.

She had forgotten how well known Ryan must be in the town as a paediatric surgeon and a very attractive single father, and every time someone called across to him in greeting, she was observed with unconcealed curiosity.

In keeping with the frosty winter morning she was wearing a designer winter coat, elegant knee-high boots with high heels, and on her head was a fake fur hat the same colour as the coat. She wondered if the interest she was arousing in passersby was due to Ryan being seen with a woman, and an expensively dressed one at that.

Those observing them couldn't be expected to know that she had a wardrobe full of expensive clothes in a house that was like something out of the Dark Ages except for one room. Before leaving it, she'd stood in front of the mirror in the dressing table that had been one of the few things she'd managed to salvage from the onslaught of the bailiffs, and thought that if she sold some of her clothes, the money would buy wall-paper and paint.

Ryan had also noticed the stares and buzz of inter-est they were causing and suggested they go down the next side turning, but she shook her head and told him she was fine. She wished it was true.

While they drank coffee and the children sipped hot fruit drinks, Melissa and Ryan were silent. The girls, unaware of any tension in the atmosphere, chat-ted happily about their role in the upcoming wedding and Rhianna asked, 'Will you help us to get dressed that morning, Melissa?'

'Er, yes, of course I will, if you want me to,' she answered, somewhat dazed at the way she was being involved in their lives once more. She wasn't sure how Ryan would feel about her stepping into the mother role once again, so having offered to do as Rhianna had asked she needed to know what his opinion was.

'Would that be all right with you? I don't want to intrude on such a special day.'

'Of course. I would be greatly obliged if you would help the girls to get dressed, but only if you come to the wedding as my guest.'

'All right, I'll come!' she said levelly. 'Are you sure you want me at the wedding as your guest, though? It always feels like treading on eggshells when we are together outside the hospital. When we're there it's so different, more like being on safe ground.

'I've got to go, Ryan. I'll come for the children at the

arranged time this afternoon.' And after kissing them both lightly on the cheek, she left the café.

Ryan sighed. Melissa had kisses in plenty for his children, but no tender gestures came his way.

They worked together as if they were joined at the hip, but once away from Heatherdale Children's Hospital the spark that he'd thought was there never seemed to burst into flame. She was right to point out that things were far from easy between them outside work.

Her outfit today had been stunning but he'd hesitated to tell her so as he seemed to have developed a talent for saying the wrong thing where Melissa was concerned. His mind went back to the night when she'd opened the door of the cold, grim house next door to his, looking on the point of collapse, and had burst into tears. He hadn't known in those few seconds that his life was about to change. It was something he was finding hard to accept and until he did there would be no peace in him.

Now that Melissa had gone, the children were fidgeting, ready to go. He paid for the drinks and they set off in the same direction as Melissa. He was hoping they might draw level with her, but she was nowhere to be seen and he wondered how she could move so fast on those heels.

Melissa enjoyed the afternoon spent with Mollie and the children immensely.

Melissa liked Ryan's middle-aged housekeeper and had not forgotten how she had suggested to him that they invite her to eat with them in her distressed state on that dreadful night when she'd been so much out on a limb she'd been on the verge of collapse.

It was easy to see that the children were fond of her, which was not surprising with Mollie being the only womanly figure in their lives.

As they walked the short distance to the high street she wasn't surprised when Mollie said, 'Rhianna and Martha are staying at my house tonight. They have a sleepover every few weeks. We have a lovely time and as it's always on a Saturday night there is no rush to get them to school the next morning. It gives Ryan a few hours of freedom to do whatever he pleases, which is rarely connected with socialising, I'm afraid.

'Before he lost Beth they had lots of friends and a lovely social life. During the first twelve months after she was gone there were some of the unmarried women that they knew who would willingly have stepped into her place if he'd asked them, but there was nothing further from his mind, and as far as I can see there still isn't.'

They had stopped outside a small but select department store and while Melissa would have liked Mollie to carry on talking about Ryan for ever, the older woman's thoughts had switched to dresses for her attendants.

'They have a delightful children's clothes section in this place, shall we see what is on show?'

A display of pretty long dresses in pastel colours, obviously aimed at Christmas partying for the young, immediately attracted the attention of all four of them. And after some degree of trying on, the small attendants-to-be were fitted out with dresses in a soft turquoise fabric with matching under-slips to help keep out the cold.

As they left the store Mollie asked, 'What do you think they should carry, Melissa, posies?'

'What about if they keep their hands tucked into little furry white muffs decorated with snowdrops?' she suggested.

The bride-to-be was smiling. 'Yes, indeed. They will keep their hands warm.'

'And what are you going to wear?' Melissa asked.

'I've bought a lovely dress and jacket in apricot silk.' Mollie's face took on a dreamy expression. 'And I'm delighted to say that Ryan is going to give me away. It won't be an easy day for him, with Beth not being there beside him, but I've invited him to bring a friend.'

'Yes, he's asked me to fill the gap.'

'That *is* good news! And are you going to?'

'Er, yes. I think so,' she replied. Mollie might not be so pleased if she knew the circumstances of her agreeing to be his partner for the occasion.

When they'd completed their shopping by buying soft white satin shoes for the children, Mollie said, 'Would you mind dropping off what we've bought at Ryan's house so that I can take the girls straight to my place?'

'Yes, of course,' Melissa said, and as the three of them set off in the opposite direction she heard Martha say, 'Melissa is going to help us get dressed for your wedding, Mollie.'

And Rhianna chipped in with, 'She's going to make us beautiful.'

Melissa considered Ryan's daughters beautiful already. With a slightly aching heart she set off to deliver the afternoon's shopping into their father's keeping.

CHAPTER SEVEN

WHEN HE OPENED the door to her Ryan stepped forward to take the shopping from her and then stood back to allow her to pass.

Noticing Melissa hesitate, he said, 'I've just finished catching up on a back log of paperwork from the hospital and am about to relax over a mug of tea. Can I persuade you to join me?'

She stepped inside, knowing that she wouldn't have refused the invitation if it had been a mug of castor oil he was offering.

He saw she was wearing the same outdoor clothes as she had that morning.

'Can I take your coat and your hat?'

Melissa nodded, and he stepped forward and slid the coat off her shoulders with one hand, gently removed her hat with the other and hung them carefully on a nearby coat hook.

She had become very still while he was taking off her hat and coat and when their glances held the dormant spark suddenly became a flame and instead of ushering her into the sitting room he led her slowly upstairs into his bedroom. As they faced each other beside the bed, which to him was the loneliest place on earth, she still hadn't spoken.

'Say something, do something, Melissa, please,' he said softly. 'Show me that you want me as much as I want you, or we'll let this moment pass.'

As he waited to see what she would do, Melissa began to take off her clothes, and as the dress that she'd been wearing beneath the coat slid to the floor and flimsy underwear and tights followed, she was smiling.

When she stood before him naked she spoke for the first time. 'Now *you* show me,' she said softly.

Without a second asking he stripped off and lifted Melissa onto the bed. His mouth caressed hers and the soft stem of her neck before dropping to the firm mounds of her breasts. She gave herself to him in a huge wave of wantonness, crying out as longing was appeased and delight filled her being.

But as she lay content in Ryan's arms afterwards Melissa realised that he hadn't spoken since he'd asked her to show him that she wanted him to make love to her. Raising herself up on to one elbow, she looked down at him and saw that his expression was no longer that of the man who had just possessed her, adored her and made her feel wanted. It was as if he'd pulled down the shutters.

'Ryan, what's wrong?' she asked with deadly calm. 'Clearly what has just happened between us didn't mean as much to you as it did to me.'

He didn't deny it and it was like a knife in her heart. Instead, he put her away from him gently.

'I am so sorry, Melissa. I would never willingly hurt you. I let my guard down, sought solace from you, and should not have done. It was unforgivable. When Beth was taken from me I chose a path to follow and have never diverted from it until a few moments ago. I hope you understand.'

She understood all right. What had made her think that the magic of Heatherdale had brought the man she would love for ever into her life when he had his own agenda? Was this how Ryan coped, a brief liaison with some willing member of her sex when the strain got to be too much, and then back to the life he had chosen?

The thought brought with it the urge to be gone, back to the house of horrors next door. It propelled her to her feet and in a matter of seconds she was dressed again in the clothes she had shed so willingly. Ryan made no protest, just threw on a robe and left her to it.

When she went down the curving staircase he was waiting in the hall, and lifting her coat and the fur hat off the hook where he had hung them she walked past him and out into the winter dark.

If it wasn't for her commitment to the sick children who came into their care at the hospital and the fact that she had nowhere else to go, she would be gone. Melissa drew the curtains to shut out the night of her humiliation.

She'd convinced herself that she understood Ryan's

loyalty to the memory of his dead wife, even though it did seem an awful waste of another life...*his*. But tonight he'd taken the first step towards letting the memories be just that, and as he'd made love to her she'd rejoiced at the thought, until she'd looked down at him amongst the tangled sheets of his bed, seen the look on his face, and thought she should have known better.

After a miserable night she slept late on Sunday morning. She was brought out of sleep by the bedside phone ringing. She hoped it wasn't Ryan. He was the last person she wanted to speak to.

It wasn't, but the call *was* from next door. It was Rhianna to say that Mollie had brought them back home. They wanted to try on their dresses and the rest of their outfits to show their father, so would she come and help them to dress up for him?

She'd been finding a glimmer of comfort in the thought that she would have today to gather her wits before facing him on Monday morning, but the children were unwittingly turning that into a vain hope as there was no way she would refuse their plea.

'I'll come round in twenty minutes, Rhianna.'

After showering and dressing quickly, she skipped breakfast until later and went next door. Thankfully it was Martha who answered her knock.

'Daddy is under the shower and says he will wait until we are ready before coming down.'

Was that because he wanted to get the full effect of their outfits or because he was in no rush to see her again so soon? If that was the case, he need have no worries. If it hadn't been for the affection she had for his children he wouldn't have seen a blink of her today.

They looked delightful in the long turquoise dresses with their hands inside the pretty muffs and their feet in the satin pumps, and when Rhianna called up to Ryan from the hall that they were ready, Melissa felt her mouth go dry.

The children were standing at the bottom of the curving staircase as Melissa hovered near the front door. The longing to open it and be gone was strong, but the two small girls wanted her there and there she was going to stay no matter what, until he'd seen them dressed how they would be at the wedding.

He came slowly down the stairs towards them and she swallowed hard. Her mouth felt dry, her body weak and wilting at the sight of him with the golden thatch of his hair damp against his head from the shower and the rest of him covered by a cotton shirt and shorts. Though dry-mouthed and weak at the knees, beneath it she was in control. Last night had been humiliation time once again and she'd walked right into it, but it was not going to happen again.

On the third step from the bottom, Ryan paused and, observing her standing behind the children, stony-faced said, 'Thanks for finding the time to assist in the dressing-up parade, Melissa, they needed your help.'

'Think nothing of it,' she said levelly. 'It's nice to know that I'm needed by someone.' She placed her arms around their shoulders. 'We have two pretty bridesmaids waiting to hear what you have to say about their outfits.'

He was smiling as he came down the last steps of the staircase, giving no sign of having got the message in her first comment.

'The two of you are always beautiful to me, but in these lovely dresses, with the sweet little muffs to keep your hands warm, and the dainty shoes on your feet, you will be more beautiful than ever. What do you say to Melissa for helping you to choose them and dress up in them this morning?'

'Thank you,' they chorused, and hugged her close, then went slowly up the stairs to take off their finery.

When they'd gone Ryan said, 'I imagine that coming here this morning was the last thing you wanted to do.'

'Yes, it was,' she told him, 'and now I'm going to go and have some breakfast. I won't be available for the rest of the day.'

'Of course,' he said, and after waving to the children, who were looking down at them from the upstairs landing, she left, without another look in his direction.

The thought of spending her working day doing the job she loved had always been a pleasure to contemplate each morning as she drove the short distance to the hospital, and with Ryan nearby most of the time on the wards and in surgery it had been blissful, but not so on the Monday morning after the events of the weekend. Melissa was dreading being in his presence for any length of time.

But any awkwardness between them was avoided when she arrived because, amazingly, Julian was back in circulation, still as darkly attractive as ever but thinner, looking drawn and on crutches. She came across the two men chatting beside their cars in the staff parking area.

When Julian saw her he leant against his car and waved a crutch in her direction and she went to join them.

'This is a very pleasant surprise. It's lovely to see you. Are you just visiting, or here to take up where you left off?'

'Just visiting today,' he said breezily, with his usual aplomb, 'but I'm hoping to come back on a part-time arrangement soon. The spinal unit in Manchester have worked wonders for me. The boss says he'll have me back whenever, so we will be a happy threesome once more.'

Melissa very much doubted it!

'When I'm back in harness, maybe we could have a night out together, the three of us,' Julian continued.

Melissa just smiled and didn't let it falter when Ryan spoke for the first time to comment, 'It would have to be a twosome, I'm afraid. All my time away from here is spoken for.'

On that downbeat comment he turned in the direction of the nearest entrance to the hospital and they followed him inside. Melissa took care to stay level with Julian's slow progress on his crutches and vowed that

Ryan was not going to dampen her spirits or Julian's on his totally unexpected appearance.

He didn't stay long, just enough to say hello to everyone, and when the night shift were ready to go and day staff about to take over she walked with him to his car. On the way he stopped and, leaning forward between his supports, kissed her lingeringly while they were opposite the window of Ryan's office.

Taken aback, she didn't push him away, just told him laughingly, 'It's clear that your cheek wasn't affected in the accident. You will be getting me the sack.'

'That was for the benefit of a mutual friend of ours,' he said, serious for once, 'as I guess that nothing of that nature has been happening in those quarters while I've been away.'

'The answer is *yes* and *no*,' she told him, 'but how did you pick up on that?'

'By observing you both when the two of you came to visit me in the spinal unit.'

'Oh!' she said blankly, and before he could comment further waved him off and hurried back inside.

Ryan was in the secretary's office by the time she reached the corridor, having paused briefly to remind the tranquil middle-aged woman that an urgent appointment was needed for a child who had been diagnosed with epilepsy.

The family had missed the first appointment after the diagnosis when they would have discussed the illness in detail with the parents and explained to them what treatment was going to be given their daughter to control the symptoms and seriousness of it. Ryan caught Melissa up at the entrance to the wards.

Julian's ploy had worked. He'd seen the kiss from the window of his office. His colleague had some nerve, yet why shouldn't he come on to Melissa if he was so inclined? She hadn't exactly pushed him away.

They were both free to fraternise with whoever they liked, had no family ties or emotional hang-ups from painful memories that wouldn't go away, so it made perfect sense to Ryan that Julian and Melissa would get together. It didn't make him feel any happier, though!

'The results have been back a couple of weeks from the scan I requested for a child we saw at one of the clinics with suspected epilepsy. We gave the parents a date for an early appointment as soon as we knew what it was, but they didn't keep it. So I've just been asking my secretary to phone them.' He glanced at a clock on the wall above their heads. 'So now maybe we can get the day under way.'

'Yes, of course,' she said flatly, avoiding making a fool of herself again by explaining what had been behind Julian kissing her outside his office window. There was always the chance that Ryan had been re-lieved to see her turning her attention to someone else after him bringing her down to earth so abruptly when he'd just taken her to the stars, so maybe explanations were not needed.

'I was called here late last night to observe a five-year-old boy who had been brought in as an emergency,' Ryan said. 'I want him to be our first priority this morning.'

He led the way towards a small side ward that was used for seriously ill children or any who might have something contagious.

'So what time was it when you got the call?' she asked.

'Half past nine.'

'And what did you do about Rhianna and Martha?'

'Er, brought them with me.'

'You got them out of bed to come here when I was next door?' she said in an angry whisper. 'I would have thought that their welfare was more important than you not wanting to have anything to do with me again.'

He ignored the last part of her protest and assured her, 'The children weren't asleep and they were well wrapped up with cosy dressing-gowns over their night-dresses and warm boots on their feet.

'Both of them were concerned about the sick little boy and also as I was already in the dog house where you were concerned I didn't want to damage my image any further. If you remember, you had said that you wouldn't be available for the rest of the day when you were leaving us after the girls' modelling session.

'We are not here to question each other's motives in any shape or form, Melissa. We have a very sick child here. His name is Alexander.'

They approached the small figure on the bed.

'His parents have been here all night and I've suggested that they go for some breakfast while we check if the procedure I started then is working.'

At that moment the door behind them opened and Alexander's parents appeared, followed by a porter with a trolley, and while nursing staff were lifting the small boy carefully onto the trolley Ryan said to them, 'Has Alexander had anything in the nature of a cold sore recently?'

'He had one a couple of weeks ago,' his mother told him tearfully. 'An aunt of mine who is subject to cold sores had been hugging and kissing him when she called round, and it was shortly afterwards that a big blister appeared on his lip. The chemist told us what to use and it finally healed over.'

'Let's go,' his father said impatiently, with his arm around his wife. 'There is no time to lose, is there, Dr Ferguson?' When Ryan nodded sombrely they went, one on either side of the trolley that carried their small son.

In those moments Melissa's admiration for the doctor who had even put his own children second to a very sick child belonging to someone else reached new heights. She'd had no right to criticise him for bringing Rhianna and Martha out late at night for once if Mollie hadn't been able to babysit for him, which had to have been the case.

Had she been so desperate for family and friends that she'd coveted his children? Was she now hurting because he didn't want her intruding into the life he had planned for himself and his daughters? If that *was* the case, it would not happen again.

By late afternoon their small patient was showing signs of responding to the anti-viral treatment after a second intravenous infusion. It wasn't mind-blowing, just a slight improvement, but it showed there was a chance that he might be able to fight off the serious infection, and it brought tremulous smiles to the faces of his parents that hadn't been there before.

The phone call to the family of the small girl with epilepsy had worked. A slapdash sort of young mother had brought the child to Outpatients in the late afternoon and had been forced to sit up and take notice when Ryan broke the news to her that the fits that her child had been having were due to epilepsy.

'That is the bad news,' he told her, as Melissa sat in with them. 'The good news is that young children often grow out of it as they get older. The word "epilepsy" refers to abnormalities of electrical activity in the brain that can be sometimes brief, which is how you described your daughter's seizures. Any longer and it could be a more serious matter.

'You must remember never to try to bring her out of it when she has a seizure. Just make her comfortable and she will recover of her own accord. The same if she occasionally has periods of drowsiness or doesn't answer when spoken to. Don't make a fuss, just let her come back to normality in her own time.

'A couple of things to bear in mind are to try to prevent her getting overtired or upset about anything, as those are situations that can trigger a seizure. Make sure that the staff at the school she attends are aware of the problem in case something of that kind occurs while she's in their care.

'I'm going to prescribe an anticonvulsant medicine that will help to reduce the number of seizures and in time they might disappear altogether,' he said reassuringly.

The young girl's mother had listened to what he'd had to say without interruption but now she was finding her voice and the first thing she did was apologise. 'I'm sorry we didn't keep that other appointment. I had no idea that a few funny moments in a child's life could be so serious.'

'We're hoping the episodes will decrease once your daughter starts taking the medication that I'm prescribing,' he told her.

When they'd gone Ryan said wryly, 'So what do you think the chances are that the mother will remember what I've said?'

'I'm not sure,' Melissa told him. 'She sounded sincere enough when she actually had something to say.'

'I hope you're right, for the child's sake' was the reply. 'I'm going to have a word with Alexander's parents to answer any questions they might have, and if the improvement is being sustained try to persuade them to go home and rest for a while.'

At the end of the day Ryan sought her out.

'Alexander seems to be stabilising now he's on the treatment, but in case I get called back here this evening, can we call a truce?'

'In what way?' she asked.

'Can I ask if you will stay with the girls if that should occur?'

'Yes, of course,' she said immediately. 'Just give me a buzz if you need me.' He might need her help with the girls but his requirements for her didn't seem to extend beyond that.

Ryan arrived home shortly after Melissa, and after an evening that was dominated by listening for the phone to ring into the silence, and frequently checking that his car was still where he'd parked it, Melissa went slowly up to bed.

It would seem that there had so far been no setbacks in Alexander's recovery, which was good, and also good was the thought that she and Ryan had found an uneasy kind of peace. If nothing else was ever forthcoming between them, she would have to live with the memory of being naked in his arms, matching his passion with her own, and for a few blissful moments seeing a future of living and loving together with Rhianna and Martha and maybe children of their own one day. She should have known better.

Ryan was not mercenary like David, or a shallow charmer like Julian. He was a man whose life had been changed drastically on a stormy night and he'd taken it on himself to stay faithful to his wife's memory while he brought up their children.

His life was rich and meaningful. Small wonder that he didn't need any more strings to his bow, so why did she feel that she had been guided to Heatherdale for a purpose more important than having a roof over her head?

Her grandmother had been a far-seeing woman. She'd known that one day Melissa would come to the small market town that was weaving its magic around her as it did with many others. Had the old lady foreseen her finding there the man who would be her heart's desire, while she was living in the drab town house that one day she was going to turn into a dream home?

As sleep began to claim her, her last thought was that she would seek out the place where her grandmother was buried. She recalled her father once saying that it was in the graveyard of the nearest church. When she found it she would make it beautiful, as she was doing to the house after years of neglect.

On Saturday morning Melissa set forth to find her grandmother's grave.

It was a cold and clear morning with the feeling of Christmas everywhere. The large tree that the council had erected dominated the centre of the town and shops and restaurants were in full festive mode as she walked the short distance to where she'd noticed a gracious stone building not far away from where she lived.

Older by far than the town houses, it stood on a large mound high off the roadside with a tall spire pointing upwards and was surrounded by a tranquil graveyard.

It took some time to find what she sought and her surmise that she was going to find long neglect there was proved correct. Overgrown and dirty, what had once been an attractive resting place was crying out to be cleaned, and once she'd found the spot where her grandmother was buried it would be just a short journey with cleaning materials and some hard work to make it beautiful once more. With all the weeds and brambles dug out of the ancient plot, it would be one way of offering her thanks to the person whose foresight had been her only hope to cling to in recent times.

After a quick lunch Melissa was back with all the necessary tools for the job and as she walked slowly along a side path in a sheltered place next to one of the stone walls of the church her eyes widened. There was a grave of gleaming white marble there with beautiful roses on it, but it was the inscription that caught her eye.

HERE LIES ELIZABETH (BETH) FERGUSON
CHERISHED WIFE OF RYAN
LOVING MOTHER OF RHIANNA AND MARTHA
MAY SHE REST IN PEACE

Melissa put the bucket she was carrying down slowly and laid the spade beside it. On returning to the graveyard, she'd gone down a different path to reach her grandmother's grave. If she hadn't she wouldn't have seen this. It was almost as if it had been meant, but in what way?

Yet even as she asked herself the question the answer was there. 'I don't want to take your place,' she said softly. 'I just want to love Ryan and Rhianna and Martha and help them to keep your memory alive.'

At that moment the sun broke through cloud high above and as Melissa took a last look at the beautiful memorial to a midwife who had risked her life and lost it to the elements when she'd put an imminent birth before her own safety, she bent to pick up the spade and bucket, and the rest of the things she'd brought, and at the same moment heard the crunch of feet on the gravel path in the deserted church yard.

When she looked up Ryan was coming towards her, and crazy as it was she felt as if he had caught her out in some misdemeanour as he observed what she'd brought with her in astonishment.

'What on earth?' he exclaimed, with a sideways glance at his wife's grave. 'You've not taken on an extra job at weekends as a grave-cleaner, have you? Only I'm in charge of this one.'

'That's not funny,' she said stiffly. 'The things I've brought with me are to clean up my grandmother's grave. I feel it is the least I can do after her leaving me her house.

'I came earlier to inspect it and of course after years of neglect it was how I thought it would be, so I went home to collect some things to help clean it up. I must have taken the wrong path. They all look alike.

'Your wife's grave is beautiful. I'm sure that she must have been the same, Ryan.' Melissa turned to go.

'Wait!' he called. 'Give me the spade and the bucket and anything else that is heavy. Did you honestly think I was going to let you stagger off like a pack mule?'

She didn't reply, just did as he'd asked and led the way to her grandmother's overgrown grave. 'Ugh!' he said when he saw it. 'That is too much for you to tackle. Perch on the seat over there while I give it a go.'

He was taking off his jacket and rolling up his sleeves and she said, 'Before you do, I have a couple of questions.'

'What are they?' he asked.

'Where are the children? And did you follow me here?'

'Rhianna and Martha are at a birthday party that won't be over for a couple of hours. I didn't follow you here. It was an opportunity to spend some quiet moments with Beth, to feel her near in the midst of my restricted life. I came because the future was becoming unclear and I hoped that I might see the way ahead better after some quiet time with her.'

'And I've butted into that, haven't I?' she said. 'Sallying forth with my grave-cleaning equipment. I'm sorry, Ryan.'

'You don't have to be,' he told her. 'You've done nothing wrong since the moment of your arrival in Heatherdale, except perhaps make me doubt some of my decisions. Maybe I needed someone or something to take the blinkers off my eyes.

'With regard to today and us meeting like this, I can always come again as this place is so near where I live. However, before I start cleaning the grime of ages off this imposing headstone, I have a question for you.'

'What is it?'

'Are you going to partner me, as you promised, to Mollie's wedding? Only you didn't sound too sure the last time it was mentioned.'

'Yes, I suppose so,' she told him flatly. 'If you recall the occasion of my lack of enthusiasm it was when only hours before we'd made love and I was unsure whether you had just used me because I was there or if I hadn't made the grade when it came to your sex life.'

He threw the spade down with a clatter. 'I don't have a "sex life", Melissa!

'The kind of life I live doesn't allow for that. I made love to you because you were and still are totally desirable, and you are the only woman I have wanted to make love with since I lost Beth.

'The way I behaved afterwards was because I felt guilty. Because that kind of magic didn't fit in with the vows I made when I lost her, not because I didn't want you like crazy.'

He picked up the spade. 'And now, as nothing has changed, can I proceed with the job in hand? It is going to take some time, so I will have to keep an eye on the graveyard clock with regard to the birthday party.'

So Ryan *had* wanted her. To hear that was joy untold, or at least it would be if he hadn't finished what he'd had to say with a reminder that nothing had changed with regard to his commitment.

'Don't be late on my account,' she told him, bringing the moment back to reality. 'There's no rush with this. I shall persist until my grandmother's grave is returned to its original splendour. With regard to the party, I could pick the children up if you want me to.'

'It would be good if you could,' he replied. 'They will be pleased to see you and I can carry on here until the light fades. The party is at the house of one of Rhianna's school friends and Martha was included in the invitation.'

'What time do you want me to pick them up?' she questioned. 'I'll need directions on how to get there, not being a native of this beautiful place. I can't believe what I ever saw in life in the big city.'

He rested on the spade for a moment and with his vivid blue gaze observing her said, 'So you have no regrets at finding yourself living in Heatherdale?'

'No,' she said gravely. 'I am employed in the kind of work I've always wanted to do, with a first-class paediatric consultant to learn from in the process of healing sick children, and have a house that has twice as much character even in its present state as the over-the-top expensive showpiece that was in keeping with my father's vision of an ideal home.'

She didn't mention that she might also have found the man of her dreams living just next door, too.

Ryan's glance was still on her in the silence that

followed and she brought herself back down to earth by saying, 'So, when do you want me to pick up the children and where? It will be dark soon so it would be better to go now, I feel. I'd rather to be too early than too late.'

'Yes,' he agreed, and gave her the address where the party was being held and directions to get there.

'I'll take your tools home with me and see you back there later.'

As he watched her go, snug against the cold in a warm jacket and leggings with a woolly hat covering her head, he saw a different vision of her in his mind's eye, looking up at him from the covers of his bed, beautiful, wanton, adoring. What had he done?

Spoilt it, made her feel cheap because of the self-sacrificing dogma that he lived his life by. The children had more sense than he had. They already loved Melissa without any reserve. But their life with their mother had been short, while his love for Beth had been there since his early teens and it had deepened with every passing day. Never once had he expected that they wouldn't grow old together.

CHAPTER EIGHT

WHEN RHIANNA AND Martha came tripping out of the party with all the other young guests their faces lit up when they saw her, and as Melissa hugged them to her it was a moment of unexpected pleasure in the approaching dusk of a winter afternoon.

'Where's Daddy?' Martha wanted to know, and when Melissa had explained they climbed into the back of the car and talked about the party, Mollie's wedding, and Christmas all the way home. Melissa wished that *she* could visualise some joy coming her way in the weeks to come.

When they arrived back at home, Ryan had returned and had hot drinks waiting for the three of them. With the children perched one on either side of him, he was listening intently to their excited account of the party while Melissa observed the three of them bleakly.

They had something that she was not likely to ever have, a loving family bond, because she had fallen in love with Rhianna and Martha's father. He was the only man she would ever want to give her a child and as the chances of that were not good, childless she would stay.

'You look very serious,' Ryan said suddenly from beside her. 'If it's about the grave, a few more hours the first chance I get we'll have it sorted.'

The grave was the last thing on her mind but thanks were due for his assistance.

'I'm most grateful for you taking over,' she told him stiltedly. 'Any improvement will be better than it was and, now, if you will excuse me, I need to change out of these clothes into something less drab than my grave-cleaning outfit.'

'Yes, sure,' he agreed, and it was there again, the memory of when he'd made love to her, taunting him, reproving him for how he'd treated her afterwards.

The hospital was already full of Christmas cheer, with a beautifully decorated spruce in the grounds and another in the entrance hall, and for the staff there was a ball arranged to take place a couple of weeks before.

Julian was hoping to be mobile enough to attend and was expecting an enthusiastic response from Melissa at the news, but as far as she was concerned if Ryan wasn't going to be there because of his domestic duties, or for any other reason, it would put a blight on the occasion.

With Christmas being so near, Melissa was turning her thoughts to presents for the children next door and a wedding gift for the bride-to-be. With regard to Ryan it would be like trespassing into his privacy to buy a personal gift, so it would have to be something basic that didn't give off any messages other than Christmas good wishes.

From his manner after those never-to-be-forgotten moments when he'd made love to her it had been clear that he'd felt it vital to point out that it had been just a moment of hunger for her that had been the cause of it. With the hurt of that forever in her mind he need have no concern that she was going to use the magic and romance of Christmas to tempt him again.

She smiled a wintry smile. What were the least personal of gifts for the opposite sex? Socks, scarf, handkerchiefs, toiletries, book token?

What about a romp with a junior doctor? From the way he'd described it, there had been nothing personal about *that*, either.

On the Friday night before the staff ball Melissa went shopping, and as she walked past the house next door on her way to the town centre it was ablaze with light. The curtains were drawn back and she could see Ryan and children seated at the dining table, having their meal. Longing swept over her in a painful tide as any impetus to shop drained away at the sight.

For a moment she almost turned back, but returning to her empty house would make the evening seem even more desolate. Better to be among the crowds of late-night Christmas shoppers than cooped up on her own.

It turned out to be the right thing to do. The shops were ablaze with all the reminders of the time of year they could think of, and inside them the public were buying gifts that would be brought out into the open only on the day.

Choosing a present for Mollie was no problem. A wedding gift voucher from the elegant department store where they'd chosen the girl's dresses didn't take long, and neither did a talking teddy bear each for Rhianna and Martha.

About to take the escalator to the floor above that to Menswear, she stopped, her eyes widening.

Ryan and the children had been on the point of finishing their meal when Melissa had passed the house earlier looking less than happy, and he had immediately gone into the kitchen where Mollie was tidying up and said, 'I've just seen Melissa go past looking lost and lonely. Could you hang on here for a little while longer, so that I can go after her to make sure that she's all right?'

'Yes, of course,' she said immediately. 'That lovely girl has nobody else to care about her except us. Take as long as you like.'

'All right, no need to push it, Mollie. I *have* got eyes in my head, you know.' He opened the front door. 'I'm presuming she was off to do some late-night shopping, would you agree?'

'Almost certainly' was the reply. 'The shops are open late tonight. Try the department store where we shopped for the girls' outfits. It's classy and so is she!'

Groaning at Mollie's second plug in favour of the

only woman he'd ever cared about since Beth had been taken from him, he went, heading off towards the town centre.

There was only one man that she knew with hair like gold and eyes as blue as a summer sky. Melissa watched Ryan making his way towards her through the crowds. But how could that be? It was only a short time since she'd seen Ryan and his children having their evening meal.

He was beside her in seconds, relieved to have found her so quickly. Taking her arm he drew her to one side. Observing him anxiously, she asked, 'What's wrong? I saw you eating at home not long ago.'

He was smiling. 'That was then, this is now. I saw you pass and thought you looked lost and lonely so I followed you to make sure that you were all right.'

She felt tears prickle her eyes. He cared enough to come chasing after her from just a fleeting glance through the window, but not enough to want her in his home, his bed and his heart. *She* knew where she belonged but he didn't.

'I'm fine,' she told him with a brittle smile. 'I came to do my Christmas shopping for the only people I know as I'm short on family and friends. I also came to get a wedding gift for Mollie and Jack. I take it she's with Rhianna and Martha?'

'Yes, of course,' he told her evenly, and wondered if Julian was on her list. If what he'd seen outside his office window that day was anything to go by, he might have graduated to the top of it. But for the present the moment was his. He'd found Melissa, and Mollie had said there was no need for him to rush back.

'Let me take you for a coffee,' he suggested, 'or we could be more upmarket and go to a wine bar. I'm not too pushed for time.'

She was wearing the fake fur hat and coat again and was very much the elegant shopper, but there was strain in her expression, her dark hazel gaze was asking for answers to the questions that filled her mind and without setting too much store on his importance in her life he knew that he was most likely the cause of it.

'Yes, all right,' she agreed, to his surprise. 'Whatever you decide will be fine.'

'We'll go to a new place that has just opened near the pump room. I was there the other night and it is quite something.'

He'd seen her expression and said, 'It was on a private consultation. The guy and his wife who own the place are the son and daughter-in-law of the chairman of the hospital board and they'd asked for a visit to their small daughter in their apartment above the wine bar. So, you see, I wasn't living it up,' he said dryly. 'Mollie was doing the honours once again and I nearly asked you to go with me for the experience... and the company.'

'But you didn't,' she commented, as they made their way out of the store amongst the jostling crowds.

'No, I didn't. It was Tuesday night and it had been an

exhausting day for us both, if you remember. It hardly seemed fair to ask you to work on into the evening.'

It was only half-true. It had been on his mind to ask her to accompany him ever since the chairman's urgent phone call that morning. He only felt alive in her presence, and when she wasn't there he lived on the memory of her in his arms, giving herself to him trustingly, completely, only to be rejected when his sanity had returned.

And then, hoping to lessen the hurt he'd caused her, he'd got himself involved in the task of cleaning up that filthy grave with Beth's beautiful white marble gleaming not far away in a wintry sun. He doubted it was enough to earn her forgiveness.

He was steering her across the busy main street with his hand beneath her elbow and as she looked up at him questioningly he said, 'What?'

'The little girl you went to see, what was the problem?'

'I'm not sure until I get the results back from tests that I've arranged. There was something rather puzzling about her condition.'

'So are you going to tell me what you think it might be?'

'No. This is the two of us spending a short time together away from everything else in our lives.'

'We won't be away from everything if the little girl's parents are at the wine bar,' she pointed out.

He shook his head. 'They won't be. They're staying the weekend at the grandparents' place, the chairman's house. Otherwise I wouldn't be taking you there as it would seem rather tasteless, don't you think?'

'Yes, I do,' she agreed, and thought it would also be tasteless if Ryan was using their meeting in the department store as an opportunity to spare her some of his precious time, with the get-away excuse, whenever he chose to use it, of Mollie waiting to be relieved from childminding.

He had stopped outside what had to be the wine bar. Soft lights were spreading their glow onto the pavement outside another of Heatherdale's attractive stone buildings and she hoped that it wasn't going to be one of those places with low lighting and intimate corners.

It wasn't. When they went inside it was warm, well lit, and crowded. He saw her smile and thought that at least one of them was pleased.

When he'd gone through the bar area on the Tuesday night to get to the apartment above, it had been deserted, but tonight was Friday of course. 'Shall we go somewhere else?' he suggested, not wanting to forego the pleasure of some quiet time together that they weren't going to get in that place.

'No,' she told him. 'Maybe just the one drink and then home.' She glanced at the shopping that he'd been carrying for her. 'We're not exactly dressed for Friday night on the town and Mollie needs to be relieved. I'll stay with the children while you take her home.'

He almost groaned out loud. Having got her to himself for once, Melissa was all for rushing back home. She'd been wary of being alone with him ever since they'd made love. Was there ever going to be any clarity in their lives away from the hospital?

Workwise they were in complete harmony, both with the same dedication, but away from that there was nothing to hold on to. He wasn't going to let the opportunity to talk about themselves go by, even if only for a short time, and when they'd found a table and he'd been to the bar Ryan asked, 'Would you like to spend Christmas Day with us, Melissa? The children would love it, if you haven't already made other arrangements.'

She smiled a twisted smile. What other arrangements could she have made in a place where she knew no one and had no connections other than those she worked with? The alternative would be booking a solitary meal at some restaurant.

'It's very kind of you to invite me,' she said stiffly, 'and I would love to be with the children on such a special day, but I wouldn't want the invitation to be a drag on you personally at a time that will have painful memories.'

'Having you with us will help to put them into the right perspective,' he told her, and was amazed how much he meant it. 'So what do you say?' He smiled. 'Would you be willing to sample my cooking?'

'Yes, I would,' she said. 'I really would. I'd love to spend Christmas Day with your children.'

She hadn't mentioned looking forward to spending the day with him but between now and then he would work on it, just as long as he didn't allow himself to be sidetracked by responsibilities that he was hesitant about sharing with anyone else.

With a lighter heart than when he'd found her in the department store he said, 'Maybe we should make tracks. As you so rightly pointed out, we ought to be relieving Mollie.'

As they walked the short distance to their respective houses there was new harmony between them that Melissa prayed would last, and that she wasn't setting herself up for more heartache.

They found the children asleep and Mollie painstakingly retrieving dropped stitches in Rhianna's knitting when they got back. On seeing their expressions, the older woman thought thankfully that the short time they'd spent together seemed to have brought them closer.

When he came back after seeing Mollie safely home, Melissa was ready to leave, and he protested, 'Surely you have time for a coffee?'

She was turning to go and shook her head. 'I have things to do, Ryan.'

'I'm still not forgiven for what happened between us, am I? Our working relationship is second to none, but our private lives are lagging behind, and I'm to blame but, Melissa, I *am* working on it.'

She was weakening. 'It isn't your fault that you lost the wife that you loved so much, and your devotion to her memory is very special. But what about your children's needs? Do you remember what Rhianna asked Santa for?'

'Yes. I am hardly likely to forget that. She asked for a *mummy*, which was not the first time since you came into our lives, but I'm not going to fill the gap for the sake of my small daughter's request to Santa. It is the agony of such a loss that I couldn't face again that makes me hesitate. *Do you understand?*'

She was across the room and holding him in her arms. 'Yes, I do,' she told him softly. 'It would be so much easier if I didn't, but I do.'

Brushing her lips gently across his cheek, she held him closer and when he turned his head the kisses were there and everything became a blur of aching need until he eased himself out of her arms.

Looking down at her gravely, he said, 'I don't want to hurt you any more, Melissa. I'm going to make that coffee and afterwards I'll see you safely back to your place.'

She nodded, unable to speak because her heart was racing and her bones melting as he disappeared into the kitchen.

When he came back with the drinks Ryan said surprisingly, 'Am I right in thinking that our friend Julian lusts after you? I saw that kiss out there in the hospital car park and let's face it, *he* wouldn't bring any baggage with him, would he?'

'That was Julian trying his hand at matchmaking between the two of *us*, instead of his usual womanising,' she informed him with the euphoria of previous

ABIGAIL GORDON   149

moments disappearing. 'I do not sleep around with
the likes of him, neither do I like to be described as
husband-hunting, and if ever you decide that we do
have a future together I would feel blessed to have
Rhianna and Martha to love and care for, just in case
you have any issues about that.'

She was on her feet and placing the coffee cup carefully on to a nearby table when she said, 'I can see myself out.' As he came towards her she shook her head
and before he could protest she was gone.

Saturday dragged by with the thought of the ball in
the evening bringing no feeling of anticipation. If it
wasn't for the fact that Julian was to be there and expecting a fuss from everyone at his reappearance, Melissa would have given it a miss. She couldn't even
muster the enthusiasm to come up with an outfit for
the evening ahead.

One thing she wasn't short of was clothes, expensive
ones that she'd been loath to part with when settling
her father's debts. Her smart car, her jewellery had all
gone into the seemingly bottomless pit, but her clothes
she'd managed to save and somewhere amongst them
were a couple of evening dresses carefully protected
against the chill that was ever present in her grandmother's house.

They hadn't discussed the ball since his put-down
after they'd made love. When it had been mentioned
before then it had seemed that it was one occasion

when he was prepared to socialise and let his children do one of their favourite things—spend the night at Mollie's.

So she had half expected that they would go together for the sake of convenience if nothing else, but things had changed between them since then and if he suggested they go together now she would refuse. There was no point in starting hospital gossip when there was nothing to comment about.

She was going to go use a taxi to transport her there and back. That way her arrangements could be best controlled. The thought of an early departure might seem tempting as the evening wore on.

When she tried on the dresses the choice wasn't easy. A black low-cut number that fitted the smooth lines of her body like a glove or a high-necked sleeveless dress of pale cream silk that accentuated the dark sheen of her hair and luminous hazel eyes were the choices before her.

She was drawn towards the black with an urge to show her neighbour that she was more than the drab girl next door, much more.

But the jewellery sold to help clear the debt had left her without the kind of relief that the black dress would need, whereas the cream number's high neck needed no such adornments.

So putting the thought of sophistication to one side, when the time came to dress for the evening ahead her choice was going to be that with long elbow-length gloves to match the dress and conceal her lack of finery.

* * *

After the rebuff of the night before, Ryan had spent the day cleaning the car in the morning and then taking the girls to the cinema to see a children's Christmas movie in the afternoon. Mollie had been to collect them and a brooding silence lay over the house.

There had been no sightings of Melissa all day and as the minutes dragged past he knew that he could not let her make her own way to something like the ball in the town centre when she hardly knew the place.

It would be churlish not to offer to take her. If she refused, so be it, but at least he would have offered, and if she preferred to spend the evening with Julian and his cronies he would have to endure it because she must be weary of him forever bleating about his responsibilities.

When she opened the door to him his eyes widened. He had yet to shower and change into a dinner suit, but she was ready, beautiful, and desirable in a fantastic dress.

'I came to ask how you intend to get to the ball,' he said levelly.

'Why? I'm going by taxi. I was just about to ring for one,' she replied, hiding her dismay at the sight of him showing no sign of being ready himself. Was Ryan not going because she was?

'Forget the taxi,' he said. 'I'll take you.'

'No, thanks.' As his jaw tightened, she continued, 'You might cramp my style while I'm giving all the men with no baggage the benefit of my company, and in any case if you are driving it will stop you from drinking a toast or any other kind of alcohol.'

'So why don't we share a taxi, if you don't mind waiting until I'm ready?' he persisted.

'Yes, all right,' she agreed, relieved to know that he hadn't changed his mind about the evening ahead, that he still had every intention of attending the ball.

When he called for her half an hour later her mouth went dry at the sight of him, as it always did. Scrubbed clean with his golden fairness accentuated by a dark dinner jacket and pristine white shirt, he was every woman's dream man yet didn't seem to realise it, and if he did, he didn't care.

In that moment it was there again. The certainty that she would never want any man but Ryan, and if he didn't feel the same about her she was either going to have to stand by and watch him live his life without her or leave Heatherdale and endure a second new beginning where he wasn't forever so near but so unattainable. With that thought came the vision of a grave of beautiful white marble in a secluded corner of a nearby churchyard.

'I rang for a taxi before I left the house so it should be on its way,' he informed her, conscious that her thoughts were somewhere else, though he would have been surprised to discover where.

They sat facing each other on the drive to the hospital, each of them so conscious of the other they needed the space between them to quell the longings they sparked off in each other.

When they arrived at their destination, Melissa stood by hesitantly while Ryan paid the taxi driver. She was the one who should have given the ball a miss. It would have been so much easier for them both if she had.

He belonged there, was highly respected at the hospital, and had lived in Heatherdale all his life. She was a newcomer, also a doctor dedicated to child care but way behind him in experience, and with a past that when she looked back on it seemed so empty and fruitless she couldn't believe how she had existed without what she had found here.

As the taxi began to pull away, Julian's car stopped beside them at the kerb edge en route for the hotel car park. 'Wow!' he said when he saw her. 'Aren't you the lucky one, Ryan? I'm no longer on crutches but still need two sticks so I can't offer any competition.' With that he drove off to find a parking space.

'One can't help but admire that guy's impudence,' Ryan said laughingly when he'd gone. 'Can we stand having him back when he's well again, do you think? Julian has already been sounding me out with regard to some part-time hours, but I don't relish the idea of him hovering over you all the time to make me jealous.'

Melissa hadn't spoken since they'd arrived. Julian's appearance had lifted her out of the doldrums, but she was still not in a party mood and had no answer forthcoming to what Ryan had just said.

Instead, she led the way into the foyer and when they separated to go to their respective cloakrooms to hand over their coats she realised that this must be a rare occasion for Ryan, out on the town probably for the first time in ages.

She was wrong not to understand his lifestyle, and wrong to present such a miserable face. Tonight she would forget everything except that she loved him more than life itself, and if she possibly could was going to make it a night for him to remember.

When she appeared back in the foyer he was chatting to an older couple she identified as the chairman of the board and his wife.

As she hesitated Ryan beckoned her across.

'Dr Redmond is a colleague who has recently joined us and is proving to be a lifesaver in every sense of the word. She will be working with me as I treat your granddaughter.'

Ryan must have received the results of the test he'd ordered. She was keen to discuss the findings, but other guests were hovering, waiting to speak to the chairman of the hospital board, and as the two of them moved on she asked, 'So what is it that is wrong with their granddaughter?'

'I only got a phone call with the results of the tests a few moments before I left the house tonight,' he explained, 'and have just been informing the grandparents of what has come up in them before I told you. Are you sure that you want to talk work at a time like this?'

'Yes, if you do.'

'Then let's find somewhere where we won't be overheard. This is a private consultation that I'm dealing with, don't forget.'

'I won't forget,' she promised. Their work with children with neurological problems was the one area of their relationship that brought no personal heartache.

'Have you heard of von Recklinghausen's disease?' he asked when they were seated at a table at the far end of the ballroom. 'Or to give it its medical title neurofibromatosis?'

'Only vaguely.'

'I'm not surprised with a name like that. It's an inherited disorder diagnosed from numerous soft fibrous swellings of nerves on the trunk and pelvis in the first instance. They can be of any size and are pale brown in colour.'

'And that is what the little girl has got?'

'Yes. Fortunately they are not present in the central nervous system, which could cause problems such as epilepsy. They will not require surgery unless they begin to look unsightly.

'When I said I was confused as to whether I was right in suspecting the von Recklinghausen's disease it was because no one in either of the child's parents' families has ever had it, so little Carly seems to be what could be the first of others who might inherit it from *her* if she has any children.

'Her grandparents have been extremely worried about her and even now with a diagnosis that might have been much worse they're apprehensive. I've told

them that we will see her regularly and keep a keen eye
open for any signs of the illness affecting the central
nervous system in the future, and there you have it.'

At that moment an announcement was made asking those present to take their places for the meal that
was part of the evening, and as they seated themselves
with the rest of the neurology staff Julian appeared on
the other side of her.

'I saw the two of you wrapped up in each other at
the far table,' he murmured conspiratorially.

'We were discussing a patient, if you want to know,'
she told him. 'Don't jump to conclusions.'

CHAPTER NINE

As THE NIGHT wore on Melissa was conscious of the festive atmosphere amongst the staff of the renowned children's hospital. It was an opportunity that came once each year for them to socialise with those who, like themselves, worked endlessly towards the healing of the young.

Obviously a few were missing because the wards and emergency sections needed to be staffed, as well as having a small nucleus of theatre staff available should the need arise, but the bulk of them were there to enjoy the Christmas ball that the authorities held for them each year.

It had been noted by most of them that Ryan Ferguson, head of the neuro unit, had arrived in the company of his new registrar, and there were those there who were curious as to the meaning of it. But when she was swept in turn onto the dance floor by a couple of young medics, with an amicable smile from the man himself, their interest waned.

Fortunately, they were not able to read his thoughts,

which were a jumble of not wanting to be seen to be monopolising Melissa and the longing to hold her close and dance every moment of the night away with her. But she'd reminded him about his tactless comment regarding men with no baggage and he was giving her the chance to get to know some of them.

For her part, she'd felt sick inside at being handed over to the young hopefuls like some sort of raffle prize, and when they had each returned her to where Ryan was chatting to other staff members, she was already debating whether to go and keep a subdued-looking Julian company to make up for his lack of mobility.

No sooner had the thought occurred to her than she acted on it and as Ryan watched her cross the now deserted dance floor in that direction he groaned inwardly.

He wanted her in *his* arms, not those of someone else, to be able to forget his hangs-ups and frustrations for a while. So why wasn't he doing just that, letting Melissa's nearness banish the aching feeling of loss that was there whenever they were apart?

'So what's new?' Julian asked, when Melissa seated herself beside him. 'Is the boss blind or what?'

'I'm competing against a beautiful memory,' she told him, 'and I don't want it to be like that. I want Ryan to see me as an opportunity to move into a new relationship without causing any hurt to the past, but of all things he is a man of honour and integrity. He was the first person I met when I came to Heatherdale and he took my breath away.'

'That was because you hadn't met me first,' he teased, and as she laughed at his cheek he went on, 'Watch out, here he comes.'

The band had started to play again, smooth, languorous music to warm the blood and create desire. When Ryan stopped in front of them he held out his hand, and when she took it in hers he raised her to her feet and said, 'My turn, I think.'

It would always be his turn if he could only see the rightness of it. More likely he was only dancing with her out of some sense of duty.

She was wrong about *that*! Ryan stayed by her side for the rest of the evening. Every time the music filled the ballroom they danced and his nearness was fantastic, his touch a delight. She wondered how the night would end for them, with the children safely tucked up at Mollie's.

It wasn't going to be her in his bed, that was for sure. The pain of his rejection after they'd made love still gnawed at her. So what did it leave them, a peck on the cheek and goodnight?

Unaware of her confusion, Ryan was smiling down at her. They were being watched, talked about, and he didn't give a damn. He could imagine them gossiping about him and Melissa, but for once Ryan didn't mind.

He had gone to the bar to get them drinks and while he was waiting to be served amongst many others Melissa's unease increased regarding what was going to happen when they arrived back home with only them-selves to be concerned about.

They'd danced almost every dance together; the at-traction between them was at its peak. Would they be able to separate each to their own property with just a brief farewell?

She wouldn't be able to face another putdown if they made love, only for Ryan to have regrets again after-wards. It was a ghastly situation to be in, never sure whether one day he would ask her to marry him, or would keep her on the edge of his life for ever.

There was the memory of the other day when they'd met unexpectedly by his wife's grave and he'd made no secret of how much Beth still meant to him. Would *she* ever mean so much to him that he could accept her in Beth's place?

The uncertainties of the moment were crowding in on her and aware that it would still be a few minutes before Ryan was served, she rose to her feet. Moving swiftly in the direction of the cloakroom, she collected her coat and keeping out of sight went into the hotel foyer and out into the night where taxis were lined up in readiness for transporting homeward-bound rev-ellers. It took only seconds to give directions to the driver of the first one in the queue and she was gone.

When Ryan arrived back at the table and she wasn't there he expected her to reappear any moment, but as the minutes ticked by and eyes were on him it began to register that Melissa was no longer in the building.

Julian stopped by the table and said, 'I think she's gone, boss.'

Ryan got slowly to his feet and made his way towards the taxi rank.

Was she insane? Leaving the warmth and safety of the hotel to go out into the dark winter night alone? Surely Melissa wasn't so wary of him that she was concerned that he might want a repeat of that last time when Rhianna and Martha had been at Mollie's?

All he had wanted was to have her with him at the ball, to dance with her, delighting in her nearness that always kept the loneliness he lived with at bay, and to see her safely home when it was over. Any other desires would have been kept tightly under control, but it would seem that she saw him as someone who would want it all his way and she'd panicked and gone.

When the taxi driver pulled up at the bottom of his drive Ryan saw that Melissa's house, gaunt and unpainted, was in darkness, and as the man drove off he wondered what to do next. How was he going to find out if Melissa was safely home or elsewhere without creating a disturbance?

One thing was sure: he was not going to put his key into the lock of his front door until he was sure that she was warm and safe behind hers. So first a phone call and if there was no answer it was going to be a case of hammering on it until Melissa appeared, and if she didn't he shuddered to think what he would do.

Melissa was huddled under the bedcovers when he rang and cringed at the sound, but when it continued she reached for the bedside phone and managed a weak 'Hello?'

'So you're back safely,' he said flatly, as relief washed over him. 'What was behind the sneaky Cinderella performance? You could at least have let me know that you wanted to leave so that I could have seen you safely home.'

'I didn't want you to have to do that,' she explained awkwardly. 'It wasn't as if I was your partner for the evening, even though we'd danced a lot. We'd just shared a taxi to take us there, that was all. I'm sorry if I caused you any anxiety, it was just that…' Her voice trailed away and into the silence that followed he let her see that he read her mind.

'You didn't want to risk a repeat of the last time the children stayed at Mollie's?'

'Yes, that was it, and now will you please leave me alone?'

'If that is what you want, yes,' he said coolly, and rang off.

Melissa turned her face into the pillows and wept.

She awoke the next morning with head aching and face red and blotchy from weeping, but with a decision made to leave Heatherdale, to find somewhere where she could live without hurt and insecurity and where there was a position in paediatrics.

Estate agents were open on Sundays for a few hours in the town, so she decided that later in the morning she would make an appointment for one of them to come round to value the house and set things in motion.

She just hoped that Ryan wouldn't make a fuss about her departure from Heatherdale when the time came.

A move in February or early March was not far away and wouldn't leave it too long before she went. In the meantime she wouldn't get any closer to Rhianna and Martha so that they weren't too upset when Santa didn't bring them a new mummy, or at least the promise of one.

And what of their father? She knew Ryan wanted her but in what role in his life? She'd been betrayed by her own father, discarded with all speed by a shallow fiancé, and in the wonder of meeting a man like Ryan had hoped that he might feel the same about her. Maybe a part of him did, but there were side issues, grief of long standing and children to consider. Would he ever feel ready to put someone in Beth's place?

Mollie brought the children back in the middle of Sunday morning and immediately cottoned onto an atmosphere of gloom around their father.

'So, how was the ball?' she asked. 'Did the two of you enjoy yourselves?'

'Er...yes,' he replied unconvincingly and she didn't pursue the subject.

There was no sign of anyone from next door when Melissa set off for the centre of the town at midday. Mollie's car was nowhere in sight so she concluded that Ryan must have taken the children out for Sunday lunch. If that was the case she was grateful for it. The last thing she wanted was to meet them on her way to the estate agent's.

The place was empty of customers when she got there and a smart-suited middle-aged man sprang to attention when she went inside and asked if someone could come to value a property that she wished to put on the market as soon as possible.

'I can come now if you like,' he offered. 'As you can see, we are quiet at the moment.'

On the point of taking him up on the offer she decided that it would be better if he came some time early the following day while Ryan was at the hospital, the children at school, and Mollie wasn't around, and with that in mind left a key with him.

By the time she arrived back at the house her determination was dwindling. Was she crazy to be cutting herself off from Ryan and the children in such a hurry? Suppose no one wanted to buy the house when the 'For Sale' sign went up. It could hardly be described as a desirable residence in its present state, and what about her grandmother's wish that she should live there, and the grave that she was going to sort out?

They were things that belonged to the past, she reasoned miserably. It was the present that she was running away from.

Monday was a weird day, working with Ryan in assumed harmony when she longed to be somewhere else where there was no heartache. But the children in their care had to come first and no matter what was going on in their lives away from the hospital, when they were there it took priority over everything.

When they'd come face-to-face in the corridor on arriving he'd said, unsmilingly, 'I'm told that we have had some intakes over the weekend that are going to keep us busy, so when you're ready...'

'Yes, of course,' she'd said coolly, and presented herself on the wards within minutes to find him already examining a twelve-year-old girl who had been rushed in over the weekend after drinking some kind of noxious substance and had had to have her stomach washed out.

'Do we know what it was?' she asked.

'Not at the moment,' he replied. 'Apparently the youngster was partying at a friend's house and was given a drink that caused her to start vomiting and lose consciousness temporarily. The inside of her mouth and throat is very inflamed so she's been given something to ease that, and as you see she's now sleeping normally after the ordeal of the stomach wash-out.

'Her mother is here. She thinks that one of the lads at the party thought he was playing a harmless trick on her daughter and gave her some concoction in the drink that he'd got out of the chemistry lab at school. He is now being questioned by the police.'

His voice was brisk and businesslike, as it always was when they were on the wards or in the clinics, but there was a remoteness about it that wasn't usually there, as if he was talking to a stranger. Whatever was between them was now over.

It confirmed to Melissa that she was doing the right thing in leaving Heatherdale, and when the estate agent rang in the early afternoon with a valuation figure that was better than she'd expected she told him to go ahead with the sale.

'How about a board outside?' he questioned. 'Not everyone wants that, but it is a good way of advertising.'

'Yes, please,' she told him. It would be easier for Ryan to find out what she was planning that way, instead of having to face him herself with the news.

When she'd arrived at the hospital that morning everyone except her had chatted about the ball. There'd been no sign of Ryan and she'd gone to the secretary's office to check on what the day had in store for them to avoid being involved in the small talk when they came face-to-face.

He was still annoyed by her conduct of Saturday night, when she'd left the hotel without telling him, and if his manner was remote his feelings weren't. He'd been so wrapped up in his safe lifestyle he'd given no thought to hers, living alone without friends or family in that ghastly house. Tonight he would make amends, go round to see Melissa and ask her to forgive him for his selfishness.

That determination lasted until he pulled up in front of their two houses in the evening and saw the 'For Sale' sign. 'Oh, no!' he exclaimed. Were his eyes deceiving him?

Melissa must have really meant it when she'd told him to stay away from her. Where on earth was she planning to go? She'd told him how she loved Heather-dale. Had it been a short-lived attraction and the same applied to him? She was writing him off like a ship that had passed in the night.

And what about Mollie's wedding? He'd asked Melissa to partner him for the occasion and be there for the children while he was performing his duties during the service. Rhianna and Martha loved her and she loved them. It was just him who was the problem.

There was no sign of her car so maybe she was avoiding him. She would have to face him sooner or later and until then he was going to keep a low profile, for her sake if nothing else.

'What do you think is going on next door?' Mollie questioned when he went inside. 'Doesn't Melissa like us any more?'

'I don't think she has any problems with you and the girls,' he told her wryly, 'but she's not too thrilled with me.'

'She won't be gone before Christmas, will she?' she asked anxiously, without commenting on his remark about himself.

'I very much doubt it' was the reply. 'She won't want to miss your wedding and also hopefully the children's excitement on Christmas morning.'

He was rallying from the shock of seeing the sale board. House buying always took a few weeks at least, sometimes months, and if she got a buyer who was in no rush it could take for ever. Melissa would be around for Christmas, unless she'd got any other dreadful surprises planned.

* * *

Melissa had called in at the estate agent's just before they closed to sign any necessary paperwork and to avoid arriving home at the same time as Ryan. When she eventually turned up she breathed a sigh of relief because there was no sign of him, which would give her a few hours' respite before having to face him the following day.

Once she'd eaten she phoned Mollie, who was back home, to assure her that she would be there for her wedding and if she needed any help with anything she had only to ask. The last thing she wanted was to cause any hassle for either the bride or her two small attendants.

'I'm sorry to see that you're intending leaving us, Melissa,' the older woman said. 'Ryan and the children need you, and I feel that you need them.'

'I can't compete with his devotion to his wife's memory,' she told her. 'He is happy as he is, Mollie.'

'Not all the time.'

'Maybe, but that is how it seems to me,' she replied, and changed the subject. 'I will see to the children getting ready on the morning of the wedding so have no worries on that score, and will be in touch before then to check if you need me for anything else. If Ryan still wants me to partner him, that's okay, too, though I have my doubts about whether he will.'

After saying goodbye to the motherly housekeeper, she settled down to browse over the day's events, aware that so far there had been no feedback from Ryan.

Maybe he was just relieved that she was removing temptation out of his way.

Ryan was far from relieved about the state of affairs. If Melissa had wanted to make him realise how much she meant to him, she was succeeding. Mollie had called to say that the two of them had spoken on the phone and that Melissa was still available to assist on the morning of the wedding and that she would still partner him on that occasion if he wanted her to.

So there was going to be time for her to change her mind over Christmas and afterwards while she was waiting for a buyer. In the meantime, he would be his normal self when they were in each other's company, without referring to her wanting to move.

The next morning on the wards Ryan talked only about their patients, which was not unusual on a normal day, but Melissa had been expecting at least some mention of her putting the house up for sale and concluded that he must see it as something of minor interest. If that was the case, she wasn't going to refer to it, either.

The days leading up to Christmas and Mollie's wedding were some of the strangest Melissa had ever known. On the last Saturday before the two events there was a knock on her door and she opened it to find a van from a local tree nursery parked in front. When he saw her the driver said, 'I've got a tree here for you.'

'There must be a mistake,' she told him. 'I haven't ordered anything from you.'

'Well, somebody has,' he told her. 'Two trees were ordered and paid for to be delivered to these two houses.' When she looked across, Melissa saw that he had already deposited a tree on Ryan's drive. 'Your neighbours are out,' he explained, and without further comment went to his truck and hoisted a fresh green spruce tree from the top of a pile and carried it to her door and through into the hall.

'Have a nice Christmas, lady,' he said, after resting it upright against the wall, and went on his way.

Where she hadn't done anything regarding decorations so far, Ryan's house already had a festive look about it, with fairy lights around the door and Christmas lanterns glowing in the garden as soon as darkness fell. No doubt the delivery of the tree would create a focal point for the children's presents to be placed around.

All of that was perfectly understandable but why go to the trouble of providing her with a tree too? Was it another example of the way he was ignoring her decision to leave him to his restricted existence?

Later the same morning, on her way to buy ornaments for the tree, she stopped off at the cemetery to put Christmas flowers on her grandmother's grave, and observed it in amazement when she got there. It was immaculate. Ryan had said he would clean it and had kept his word, but how when it was dark in the evenings and late afternoons and there would be no time before he went to the hospital each morning?

It was only the previous Saturday that they'd met there and he'd made the offer. Had it been in his thoughts that he wanted her to have peace of mind regarding it when she was gone and had wasted no time in cleaning it up?

Before continuing on her way, she stopped in front of Beth's grave. She would try to make up for their mother not being there over Christmas for the children, but couldn't promise any joy with regard to their father because he didn't want her to take their mother's place and she would have to accept that.

Ryan had gone to have a haircut in readiness for his role at the wedding and had gone to a unisex hairdresser so that Rhianna and Martha could have theirs made especially beautiful at the same time in preparation for the occasion. Only a week to go and it would be upon them.

When they arrived back at the house the tree was there on the drive, but there was no sign of Melissa's. He hoped that she'd accepted it in the spirit it had been given. Whatever happened in the new year, he was determined that her decision to leave Heatherdale was not going to put the blight on Christmas.

He saw her go past on her return from the shops and within minutes she was on the phone, thanking him for the tree and asking how he'd managed to find time to finish the cleaning of the grave.

'It was just as easy to order two as one, and no way

would the children want you not to have a tree when they come to see you over Christmas. As to the cleaning up of the grave, I'm afraid I haven't been performing miracles. The church has a facility where they will maintain a grave on a regular basis, so you have your answer to that.'

'Well, thanks, anyway,' she told him. 'If you pass the contract on to me, I'll see that it gets paid when due.' And without further comment she rang off with the thought in mind that she was supposed to be keeping a low profile with Rhianna and Martha instead of spending most of Christmas with them. But it wasn't going to be easy with the wedding and Christmas morning and everything else that gave the young excitement and delight at such a time of year.

If the morning had brought surprises with it in the form of the unexpected delivery of the tree and the immaculate gravestone, the afternoon's surprise was in a class of its own.

The estate agent phoned to say that they had a buyer for the house. 'What, already?' she croaked, as her legs felt as if they would give way under her. Yet wasn't it what she wanted, to be off as soon as Christmas was over?

'Those houses where you live are always soon snapped up,' he said, 'so don't be surprised. It amazes me that they're not listed, like a lot of the buildings in the town. The buyer's bankers are in charge of the sale as he is some busy professional guy, so we'll be dealing with them.'

'When did you show him around?' she asked, still stunned.

'We didn't. He asked for a brochure to be sent to his bank, saw that it was what he's looking for, and wants to buy it. Could be a developer, I suppose,' the voice at the other end of the line was saying, and as she listened it was all so unreal, like Ryan's calm acceptance of her leaving Heatherdale with no sign of dismay.

If anything should make her feel confident that she was doing the right thing, it was that, but if she'd been lost and lonely when she'd come to this place that had captured her heart, what she was going to feel like when she left it didn't bear thinking of.

In the early evening she went upstairs and went through her clothes to decide what was going to be the most attractive outfit she possessed to wear at Mollie's wedding.

A pale blue dress of fine wool with a matching jacket and high-heeled shoes seemed a good choice, but she had no large wedding-type hat to go with it and settled for an inexpensive fascinator that was modern and youthful and shaped to show off the dark sheen of her hair.

When she observed herself in the mirror she was smiling. She was 'poor' and 'needy', she thought, but could manage a show of prosperity when the need arose and hoped that Ryan would approve of her outfit.

* * *

The following day the 'Sold' notice went up outside the house and if Melissa was expecting any revealing comments from Ryan regarding it she was disappointed. He merely commented as they arrived home simultaneously at the end of a busy day at the hospital that someone had wasted no time and left it at that, leaving her once again with the sick feeling that she was a poor judge when it came to the men in her life.

Especially when his next comment was to remind her that he would be cooking Christmas dinner and hoped she realised how much Rhianna and Martha were looking forward to her spending the day with them. There was again no mention of *his* feelings about the invitation, and she told him levelly if that was the case with regard to the children, she would be there.

But first there was the ordeal of the wedding to get through.

It was the day of Christmas Eve, and as Ryan drove the four of them through town to the church where the wedding was to take place it was thronged with last-minute shoppers and sightseers come to share in the magic of Heatherdale at a special time of year.

When she'd gone next door earlier in the morning, in good time to help Rhianna and Martha into their pretty outfits, Ryan's heart had ached when the children had run up to her and hugged her, and he'd felt the familiar longing take hold of him, as it always did when she was near.

'You look very swish,' he'd commented.

'So do you,' she'd told him, taking in the vision of the tall figure in morning suit and smart white shirt. Would she ever be able to put him out of her mind when he was no longer only feet away from her all the time at the hospital, and almost within touching distance in the house next to hers? Lots of women would be happy with that arrangement, if only to have him in their lives, but not her. The pain of always being an onlooker would be too much to bear.

The children had been tugging at her, eager to get dressed, and she'd given them her full attention for the next half-hour, then presented them to him and had to watch the pain in his expression that had to be at the thought of what their mother was missing.

She'd wanted to go to him and hold him close again, but it had been a moment that had belonged to Ryan and his children only and she'd gone into the next room and stood gazing out of the window until his voice had come from behind asking, 'So are we ready to leave, then?'

Feeling that she would be relieved when the day was over, she'd nodded and when the children had come trooping in and had stood one on either side of her she'd taken them by the hand and followed him out to the car.

The church was full of well-wishers as both Mollie and Jack were well respected in the area. Once Melissa had positioned the children behind the bride, who was holding Ryan's arm for support, the organist struck up the wedding march and the ceremony got under way, with her hurrying to find a seat near the front.

It was like the night of the ball, curious glances in her direction. Unless they'd had cause to meet her at the hospital for some reason, she was a stranger to most of them, but it would seem not so to Ryan and his children.

When she would have seated herself at a small table amongst others at the reception that followed, Ryan went to her and raising her to her feet took her to the top table to sit beside him and the children, with Mollie beaming her approval.

The bridal pair intended honeymooning in Italy for two weeks and were leaving on a flight later that evening. Ryan was taking leave due to him from the hospital to cover the time that Mollie would be away.

Fortunately she was intending to stay on in the role of his housekeeper but Melissa thought there would always be times when there was the problem of someone to be there for Rhianna and Martha when he was working. If things had been different they could have shared those kinds of responsibilities between the two of them, but he hadn't wanted to let her into his cloistered life.

No point in wishing for the moon. She had made her decision to leave behind the feeling of being surplus to Ryan's requirements, and soon would have to decide what direction to take for yet another new beginning.

CHAPTER TEN

IT WAS LATE afternoon when they arrived home from the wedding and as Melissa wished the children goodbye, with a promise to see them the next day when Santa had been, the evening stretched ahead like an empty void.

She had no wish for a continuation of the day's awkwardness between Ryan and herself, and when he'd asked her what she had planned for the evening she'd told him hurriedly that she was meeting friends in the town.

He'd eyed her dubiously and explained that he would be spending the time preparing for the Christmas dinner that he was going to cook for them the next day. She was welcome to join him if she wanted to, and if she didn't and still persisted in going into town, she must be sure to get a taxi home and to ring him if she had any problems.

'I won't be doing that,' she protested hotly, 'expecting you to leave the children on my account.'

'I wouldn't be. I would bring them with me.'

'Yes, well, that isn't going to happen because I won't need you,' she said firmly.

Under any other circumstances she would have been more than willing to be with him in the kitchen, but the thought of being alone with Ryan for any length of time, as the children would be in bed early on such a night, was not to be faced.

Never once had he said he was sorry she was leaving, that he wanted her to stay, and if that wasn't a guideline for her own attitude towards *him*, *she* didn't know what was.

He was using her fondness for his children as a lever to achieve his own ends and she couldn't believe it of him. Once Christmas was over she would be on the outside of his life, as she'd been before. Without further comment she left him to his preparations for a meal that she felt would choke her.

Melissa hadn't had any intention of going into town for Christmas Eve, but her quick-as-a-flash excuse for not spending any more time that day with Ryan was making her feel that she had to justify what she'd told him, and she *had* been invited to join a group from the hospital who were intending to wine and dine the evening away in one of the local restaurants, so maybe she would take them up on it and try to chase away the blues that way.

It didn't work. She kept thinking of Ryan and his ever-changing moods. How he hadn't wanted her to come into town, and how he'd fussed about her getting home safely, *and the rest*. Had it been that he'd felt guilty because it was because of him that she was leaving Heatherdale?

She excused herself from the gathering early and did as he had ordered and used a taxi for the return journey. She would have called to let him know she was home except that his house was in darkness and she didn't want to disturb him.

She wouldn't have done. The house lights had fused when he'd plugged the tree in and he'd been searching for a torch when the taxi had stopped in front, but he'd seen its headlamps shining in the darkness and had thought thankfully that she was back.

He had a gift for Melissa, a Christmas surprise that he would give her in the morning and hope it would last for ever, and with the lights back on, the turkey cooking slowly, and all the trimmings that went with it sorted, he went to bed, and in what seemed like no time at all the children were tugging at him to get up because Santa had been.

They'd had their breakfast and were upstairs surrounded by all the things they'd asked for when he phoned Melissa. The lights were on in the house next door, smoke was curling out of the chimney, and it was now a reasonable hour to get in touch.

When she answered he said, 'Merry Christmas. Are you up and about?'

'Er, yes' was the reply. 'I'll be over shortly. I've got presents for you and the children.' Ryan would hardly be jumping for joy when he opened his to find a book token!

'Fine,' he said, 'but I'm not phoning about anything like that. It's to tell you that the guy who is buying your house is outside and he wants a word. I think he wants to introduce himself.'

'What?' she gasped. 'It's Christmas Day, for heaven's sake.'

'So goodwill to all men, yes?'

'Mmm, I suppose so. Where exactly is he?'

'Waiting on the drive.'

'All right, thanks for letting me know.' She went to greet the stranger at her door.

But when she opened it there was only Ryan there, and looking around her she questioned, 'So where is he?'

'Quite close' was the reply. 'In fact, very close. If you reach out you can touch him.'

'What? You?' she gasped, holding on to the doorpost. 'How? Why? What do you want with two houses?'

'To make them into a home for the four of us, Melissa. Did you really think that I was going to let you go out of my life now that I've found you? Now, is it all right if I step inside? I don't want to propose to you on the doorstep,' he said gently.

Speechless, Melissa stepped aside to let Ryan in.

'When you appeared in my life on a dark autumn night, distraught and dishevelled, the last thing I felt like was having to offer you food and find you accommodation. It had been a long, busy day at the hospi-

tal and all I wanted was to enjoy the meal that Mollie
had cooked and then spend some special time with my
children. But for ever kind and thoughtful about others, Mollie wanted to see you fed and warm before I
took you to find a hotel, and I remember that I agreed
to whatever she suggested with a reluctance that must
have been obvious to you.

'I little knew that I would fall in love with the
stranger at my door and that the way of life I had set
for myself was going to be thrown into chaos. It has
taken the thought of losing you to bring me to my
senses, and I'm buying your house for two reasons.

'One, because we owe it to your grandmother. Because of her generosity in leaving it to you, you came
into my life, and because our two houses made into one
will be delightful when the builders have finished with
them. So will you marry me, Melissa? Will you let me
take you next door to tell the children that their wish
has been granted, that Santa has sent them a mummy
who will love them always?'

'Yes,' she breathed. 'It is all I've ever wanted for
weeks, to be your wife, but why buy my house when
it's yours for the asking to be part of our home?'

'Because once you were rich and now are poor,'
he said laughingly. 'And now you will be rich again.'

'Having you and the children will be all the riches
I need,' she said softly.

'Yes, I know,' he agreed, 'but nevertheless…'

With his arms around her they went to tell Rhianna
and Martha their good news, and when they ran to

her and held her close Melissa hoped that somewhere not far away their mother would be giving the four of them her blessing.

'Can we phone Mollie and tell her that we're going to have a mummy?' Martha cried

'Yes, but just a quick call,' Ryan warned, as he and Melissa went to check that the food he'd prepared was cooking satisfactorily.

In a hotel in Italy, the bride of the day before was enjoying a late breakfast with her new husband when her mobile phone rang, and when she'd listened to what the childish voices had to say she cried joyfully, 'Jack! There's going to be another wedding!'

EPILOGUE

WINTER HAD PASSED. It was spring, with new life opening up in the parks and gardens of the famous market town and with the outline of the moors that surrounded it taking on a softer green than the bleak shades of winter.

The building work was finished, the two houses had been made into one, and the result was a gracious family home that was going to be a joy to live in.

Since Melissa had come to live with them, Ryan's bed was no longer the loneliest place on earth. When he held her close in the night there was always the joy of knowing that she was his, always would be, and the spring wedding that they were planning would tell the world that it was so.

The children were on cloud nine because they were going to be bridesmaids again, this time in summery dresses with pretty posies. Julian, now recovered from his injuries, was going to be Ryan's best man, and Jack Smethurst would be giving Melissa away.

Everyone who wasn't on duty at the hospital was there to celebrate the wedding of two of its doctors, and the old stone church near the town houses was full of well-wishers, amongst them grateful parents of patients.

When Melissa arrived in a white wedding gown that was stunning in its simplicity, carrying a small ivory cross that had been her mother's and with two young bridesmaids carrying her train, it felt as if she'd been waiting for this day all her life.

When she stopped for a second, framed in the doorway of the church as the organist began to play the music that announced the arrival of the bride, Ryan turned from his position in front of the altar and as their glances met it was there, the love that each of them had for the other, and like a blessing the scent of roses, Beth's favourite flowers, was all around them.

The photographs had been taken in front of the church and as the guests began to make their way to the reception at an hotel in the town, Melissa and Ryan left the children with Mollie and Jack for a few moments and went into the graveyard. She laid the small white cross she had carried beside the roses that always graced the grave in the quiet corner then, hand in hand, they went to that other grave where Ryan placed the carnation he had worn on its weathered but immaculate surface and after a few moments in the silence that was all around them they returned to where the future was waiting.

* * * * *

Mills & Boon® Hardback
October 2013

ROMANCE

The Greek's Marriage Bargain	Sharon Kendrick
An Enticing Debt to Pay	Annie West
The Playboy of Puerto Banús	Carol Marinelli
Marriage Made of Secrets	Maya Blake
Never Underestimate a Caffarelli	Melanie Milburne
The Divorce Party	Jennifer Hayward
A Hint of Scandal	Tara Pammi
A Façade to Shatter	Lynn Raye Harris
Whose Bed Is It Anyway?	Natalie Anderson
Last Groom Standing	Kimberly Lang
Single Dad's Christmas Miracle	Susan Meier
Snowbound with the Soldier	Jennifer Faye
The Redemption of Rico D'Angelo	Michelle Douglas
The Christmas Baby Surprise	Shirley Jump
Backstage with Her Ex	Louisa George
Blame It on the Champagne	Nina Harrington
Christmas Magic in Heatherdale	Abigail Gordon
The Motherhood Mix-Up	Jennifer Taylor

MEDICAL

Gold Coast Angels: A Doctor's Redemption	Marion Lennox
Gold Coast Angels: Two Tiny Heartbeats	Fiona McArthur
The Secret Between Them	Lucy Clark
Craving Her Rough Diamond Doc	Amalie Berlin

0913 GEN STD HB

Mills & Boon® Large Print
October 2013

ROMANCE

The Sheikh's Prize	Lynne Graham
Forgiven but not Forgotten?	Abby Green
His Final Bargain	Melanie Milburne
A Throne for the Taking	Kate Walker
Diamond in the Desert	Susan Stephens
A Greek Escape	Elizabeth Power
Princess in the Iron Mask	Victoria Parker
The Man Behind the Pinstripes	Melissa McClone
Falling for the Rebel Falcon	Lucy Gordon
Too Close for Comfort	Heidi Rice
The First Crush Is the Deepest	Nina Harrington

HISTORICAL

Reforming the Viscount	Annie Burrows
A Reputation for Notoriety	Diane Gaston
The Substitute Countess	Lyn Stone
The Sword Dancer	Jeannie Lin
His Lady of Castlemora	Joanna Fulford

MEDICAL

NYC Angels: Unmasking Dr Serious	Laura Iding
NYC Angels: The Wallflower's Secret	Susan Carlisle
Cinderella of Harley Street	Anne Fraser
You, Me and a Family	Sue MacKay
Their Most Forbidden Fling	Melanie Milburne
The Last Doctor She Should Ever Date	Louisa George

0913 GEN STD LP

Mills & Boon® Hardback
November 2013

ROMANCE

Million Dollar Christmas Proposal	Lucy Monroe
A Dangerous Solace	Lucy Ellis
The Consequences of That Night	Jennie Lucas
Secrets of a Powerful Man	Chantelle Shaw
Never Gamble with a Caffarelli	Melanie Milburne
Visconti's Forgotten Heir	Elizabeth Power
A Touch of Temptation	Tara Pammi
A Scandal in the Headlines	Caitlin Crews
What the Bride Didn't Know	Kelly Hunter
Mistletoe Not Required	Anne Oliver
Proposal at the Lazy S Ranch	Patricia Thayer
A Little Bit of Holiday Magic	Melissa McClone
A Cadence Creek Christmas	Donna Alward
Marry Me under the Mistletoe	Rebecca Winters
His Until Midnight	Nikki Logan
The One She Was Warned About	Shoma Narayanan
Her Firefighter Under the Mistletoe	Scarlet Wilson
Christmas Eve Delivery	Connie Cox

MEDICAL

Gold Coast Angels: Bundle of Trouble	Fiona Lowe
Gold Coast Angels: How to Resist Temptation	Amy Andrews
Snowbound with Dr Delectable	Susan Carlisle
Her Real Family Christmas	Kate Hardy

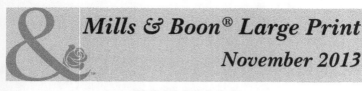

Mills & Boon® Large Print
November 2013

ROMANCE

His Most Exquisite Conquest   Emma Darcy
One Night Heir   Lucy Monroe
His Brand of Passion   Kate Hewitt
The Return of Her Past   Lindsay Armstrong
The Couple who Fooled the World   Maisey Yates
Proof of Their Sin   Dani Collins
In Petrakis's Power   Maggie Cox
A Cowboy To Come Home To   Donna Alward
How to Melt a Frozen Heart   Cara Colter
The Cattleman's Ready-Made Family   Michelle Douglas
What the Paparazzi Didn't See   Nicola Marsh

HISTORICAL

Mistress to the Marquis   Margaret McPhee
A Lady Risks All   Bronwyn Scott
Her Highland Protector   Ann Lethbridge
Lady Isobel's Champion   Carol Townend
No Role for a Gentleman   Gail Whitiker

MEDICAL

NYC Angels: Flirting with Danger   Tina Beckett
NYC Angels: Tempting Nurse Scarlet   Wendy S. Marcus
One Life Changing Moment   Lucy Clark
P.S. You're a Daddy!   Dianne Drake
Return of the Rebel Doctor   Joanna Neil
One Baby Step at a Time   Meredith Webber

1013 GEN STD LP